Gianni studied her lovely face in the low light, the lush peach curve of her lower lip as she worried at it with the edge of her teeth causing an almost blinding surge of lust to tighten every muscle in his long, lean body.

He topped up her wine and rested back in his seat, suppressing that arousal with all his strength.

"My next question has to be, are you willing to marry me to keep Ladymead in your family?" he asked levelly. "If you marry me, I will finance the restoration of the house. I will cover every necessary expense and ensure your grandmother's security and comfort."

Jo blinked rapidly and began to eat in haste, needing that simple act to ground herself again. What Gianni was offering was the fulfillment of her wildest dreams. She would be able to stop worrying, stop trying to work every hour of the day. Her family would be safe and secure.

"Gianni...you haven't thought this through—"

"On the contrary. I've thought very deeply about it."

Lynne Graham was born in Northern Ireland and has been a keen romance reader since her teens. She is very happily married to an understanding husband who has learned to cook since she started to write! Her five children keep her on her toes. She has a very large dog who knocks everything over, a very small terrier who barks a lot and two cats. When time allows, Lynne is a keen gardener.

Books by Lynne Graham

Harlequin Presents

The Greek's Convenient Cinderella
The Ring the Spaniard Gave Her

Heirs for Royal Brothers

Cinderella's Desert Baby Bombshell
Her Best Kept Royal Secret

The Stefanos Legacy

Promoted to the Greek's Wife
The Heirs His Housekeeper Carried
The King's Christmas Heir

Visit the Author Profile page
at Harlequin.com for more titles.

Lynne Graham

THE ITALIAN'S BRIDE WORTH BILLIONS

Recycling programs
for this product may
not exist in your area.

ISBN-13: 978-1-335-58402-1

The Italian's Bride Worth Billions

Copyright © 2022 by Lynne Graham

For questions and comments about the quality of this book,
please contact us at CustomerService@Harlequin.com.

Harlequin Enterprises ULC
22 Adelaide St. West, 41st Floor
Toronto, Ontario M5H 4E3, Canada
www.Harlequin.com

Printed in U.S.A.

THE ITALIAN'S BRIDE
WORTH BILLIONS

As always and with much love for the daughter who is the port in my every creative storm.

CHAPTER ONE

GIANNI RENZETTI SWALLOWED a curse when he was informed that his father, Federico, awaited him in his office. He knew what that was about, wished he didn't. But that was life and Gianni always met adversity head-on. As the phenomenally successful and youngest ever CEO of Renzetti Inc, he was determined to stand by his convictions.

His PA couldn't quite meet his eyes when she relayed the news about his father's arrival and the faintest trace of colour edged Gianni's hard-edged cheekbones, throwing into prominence the striking bone structure and stunning dark good looks that usually granted him a second and even a third glance from women. Of course, his PA would have seen the photos in the newspaper and, momentarily, Gianni was embarrassed rather than powered by the anger that had exploded in him the instant he saw that grubby article.

Here he was, evidently, labelled for life by a moment of sexual idiocy. His wide sensual mouth compressed. Yet his strongest conviction *was* that his private life—for that read sex life—was an entirely confidential matter. Unfortunately, on this particular occasion, the lines had become blurred. Gianni had been set up and he had, regrettably, succumbed to temptation in a private room at a nightclub. That had resulted in attempted blackmail and the involvement of the police followed by a very sleazy spread of photos in a downmarket tabloid. When the extortion attempt failed, the story had been sold instead.

A resigned blankness in his dazzling dark eyes, Gianni entered his office. He had always had a toxic relationship with his father. His late mother had excluded his father from her will and left her vast wealth in trust for her son and Gianni was well aware of his father's resentment on that score. What relationship the two men had had, however, had nosedived the instant that Gianni stepped into his father's shoes at Renzetti Inc. Federico Renzetti had made several poor business decisions and the board of directors, which included his father's two older brothers, had voted him out, preferring his son, who already ran a highly profitable company of his own. Although at the time Federico had insisted that he was keen to retire, his bitterness had only seemed to increase when his son had lifted the family company into the *Fortune 500* category.

'Federico.' Gianni greeted his only surviving parent with the name and formality the older man preferred and extended a stiff hand.

The older man, tall but a little portly in shape from good living, surveyed his son with tight-mouthed censure. 'I'm only here to tell you that when the board of directors vote you out at the end of the month, neither I nor your uncles will be supporting you,' he spelt out.

Gianni froze, taken aback by that declaration of intent. He had not been aware that there was any risk of him being voted out. In his experience the directors always put profit first. But evidently, the jungle drums in the family had been busily beating behind his back. A cold chill ran down his spine. Gianni cared about few things beyond work because he was the overachiever he had been raised to be. He ate, breathed, and slept business and he not only thrived as CEO of the family company, but also deeply valued his position of responsibility.

'This sordid episode has brought the company's reputation into disrepute,' Federico Renzetti ground out thinly. 'It cannot be overlooked.'

'It has brought *me* into disrepute,' Gianni contradicted steadily. 'I made a foolish misjudgement, and I won't even try to defend myself.'

'You had sex with a woman in a nightclub!' his father slashed back at him in disgust. 'With a camera on you!'

'Naturally, I was not aware of the hidden camera,' Gianni said drily. 'But neither was I willing to give way to blackmail.'

'You were in the wrong. You should've paid that scheming slut off to protect the company name!'

'Too late now,' Gianni responded, seeing no reason to argue and prolong the meeting. He saw in his father's eyes that the older man was reaping a certain amount of enjoyment from his downfall and as always that cut him deep. It made him wonder, as he so often had growing up, what he had done to deserve that lack of affection.

'You have always refused to listen to me and take my advice!' the older man denounced bitterly. 'If you kept a mistress, it would be discreet. There would be no surprises, no scandals.'

Gianni gritted his teeth because he had always believed that a mistress would be as suffocating an addition to his life as a wife. *One* exclusive woman to satisfy his every desire? Gianni enjoyed freedom and variety but even a mistress would be entitled to expect a fair degree of fidelity. Why would he sign up for that option when most of the young women he met were content to settle for a casual encounter? Furthermore, that kind of detached lifestyle reminded him too strongly of his father and he refused to make such a choice, particularly as the son of a mother who had felt humiliated by her husband's mistresses.

'Better still had you married by now and settled down!' Federico Renzetti continued grimly.

'Why on earth would I want to get married

at twenty-eight?' Gianni demanded with incredulity.

'I was a married man at twenty-three.'

'Back in the day,' Gianni scoffed, resisting a cutting urge to remark that his mother had been the richest heiress in Europe and too good a prospect for his impoverished father to pass up. 'Few adults want to settle down that young now.'

'Had you been married, even engaged, the board would have seen some sign of hope and better behaviour on the horizon for you. But you just won't grow up!' Federico told him in furious condemnation. 'What have you got against settling down?'

'Like my mother and you were so happy *settling down*,' Gianni breathed with emphatic distaste.

The older man paled at that unwelcome reminder and stepped back. 'I am sorry that you were so aware of our difficulties.'

Discomfiture filled Gianni, for he had not intended to get that personal with his parent and he rarely referred to the mother, who had died when he was thirteen. His memories of her were too private and painful. A charged silence fell for several uneasy seconds.

'Look.' Federico spread his hands in hesitant appeal. 'You could still turn this whole ghastly situation around by just choosing the *right* woman to marry. However, do you even know any decent women? You're unlikely to meet them at the raunchy private clubs and wild parties you frequent,' Federico declared with frustration. 'She would be mature and respectable, and she would have an unblemished reputation.'

'Bearing in mind the headlines I attracted over the weekend, I would imagine that a *decent* woman would be the very last one willing to marry me at the moment,' Gianni countered ruefully.

'Don't talk nonsense,' his father advised him impatiently. 'You're richer than Croesus. Even the most moral woman would be tempted by all that you have to offer…although, to be frank, she might not be tempted by your conduct.'

'And I'm not tempted by the idea of a gold-digging wife,' Gianni responded with finality. 'Let's not discuss the impossible. I can't credit that a wedding ring on my finger would silence the board's concerns.'

'We're all old men on the board, Gianni.

We equate settling down with growing up, with maturity and stability,' his father fielded drily. 'Surely even you could contemplate the picket fence if it delivers the results you want?'

Gianni gritted his teeth and said nothing. He knew party girls, bored socialites and aspiring models. But then he wasn't seriously considering his father's advice, was he? No, he wasn't. He had made a misstep and he would learn by it, even if that meant learning the hard way. He wasn't about to entangle himself in a miserable marriage to satisfy other people's moral scruples. No, not for anything, he swore vehemently.

Her fingers crumpling the letter of refusal from the bank, Josephine Hamilton stared out of the attic window towards Belvedere, the palatial mansion adjacent to her own family home. It belonged to the Renzetti family and Gianni Renzetti was the biggest landowner and employer in the area. Technically, he was also their next-door neighbour. He owned almost every scrap of ground around them and what remained was the size of a postage stamp.

Dating back to Tudor times, Ladymead, the Hamilton family home, was dilapidated. While the Hamilton family fortunes had waned, the Renzettis' fortunes had steadily risen. Over a century ago, someone on the maternal side of Gianni's family tree had bought land from the Ladymead estate to build their lavish Edwardian property. Piece by piece over the years, Gianni's ancestors had bought almost all of Ladymead's original land. Only the walled garden, the outbuildings and the strip along the lakeshore still belonged to them, she reflected sadly, wondering if Gianni would now step in like the predator he essentially was to scoop up what was left of her home once debt forced them to sell. Ladymead would sell at a knockdown price, she conceded unhappily.

Slowly descending the rickety and narrow servant staircase, idly wondering when there had last been a servant in her dusty home, she suppressed her overwhelming sense of failure before straightening her shoulders and composing her face. She had to be strong for the sake of her nearest and dearest.

Jo settled the bank's letter on the kitchen table in front of her grandmother and her two great-aunts, Sybil and Beatrix, better known as Trixie. It was a Hamilton family meeting.

'Another refusal,' her grandmother, Liz, registered in dismay, her creased and kindly face troubled beneath her halo of white hair.

'But I lit a candle for success!' Her witchy great-aunt, Trixie, exclaimed in furious disappointment, her earrings and bracelets clattering noisily, her long greying hair flying round her face as she shook her head. '*Why* didn't it work?'

The third and youngest sister, Sybil, rolled her blue eyes and lifted her false eyelashes high in true femme-fatale style. 'It didn't work because we're a bad financial bet for a loan,' she said with the innate practicality that was as much a part of her as her glamorous image. 'So, what now?'

One hand toying anxiously with the end of the long braid of her blonde hair, Jo winced, her dark blue eyes strained in her delicate pointed face. She swallowed hard. 'I've made an appointment to see Gianni and ask if he's willing to loan us the money. I've tried all the banks. He's our last hope.'

'Not sure you'll be safe seeing him alone,' Sybil quipped, referring to the shocking newspaper article that everyone local had read and devoured.

Jo ignored that crack. 'I'm seeing him this evening when he's at home for the weekend. I thought it was best to keep it casual.'

'I bet you're wishing now that you'd said yes to dinner when he asked you out again last Christmas.' Sybil sighed. 'After all, it was the *second* time he'd asked you and you rejected him. I shouldn't think those rejections will dispose him to generosity.'

'I think he would have been more shocked if I'd said yes,' Jo countered, keen to kill that subject.

Jo knew herself well and she had always refused to allow herself to be tempted by the man she suspected was probably her equivalent of Kryptonite. Gianni was the original bad boy and she had been determined not to become another notch on his heavily marked bedpost. He tempted her when no other man had contrived to do so and she was painfully conscious that she was vulnerable with him. But she had also known Gianni since she was a child and she valued even their casual friendship too much to risk losing that unique link.

'In some cultures, they believe that if you save a life, that person's life belongs to you,' Trixie mused absently. 'Gianni hasn't got much return from the effort he put in that day.'

Sybil's eyes flared. 'It didn't happen that way, even if nobody is prepared to acknowledge it. Jo saved *him* from drowning, not the other way round!' she argued.

Jo wrinkled her nose. 'I was nine years old and he was thirteen,' she reminded her great-aunts gently. 'We were both stupid and we both survived. That's all that really matters.'

Sybil parted her lips to argue and then glimpsed her eldest sister's taut face and closed her mouth again. Liz Hamilton's son, Abraham, had drowned himself in the lake and nobody liked to discuss that thorny subject around his mother.

Uncomfortably flushed by that reminder of the uneasy link she had formed with Gianni and the secret they had suppressed when they were both too young to do otherwise, Jo rose from the table. She had first met Gianni the year before that incident. Her grandmother had gone to visit his mother, who had endured a long struggle with cancer. Federico Renzetti had been less to everyone's taste than his charming, friendly wife, Isabella, who had borne her illness with such stoicism. Gianni's father had been a cold, distant man with no desire to mix in any way with the locals.

Liz Hamilton had brought roses, which Isabella had adored. High tea with all the trimmings had been served in a sunlit drawing room. Jo had been bored listening to the adult conversation and then Gianni had come in, a tall, rangy twelve-year-old with a shock of glossy blue-black hair and olive skin. Jo had seen the love in his eyes when he'd looked at his frail mother, a love that had been fully reciprocated as his mother had drawn him forward to introduce him, her pride in him patent.

He had been very polite and hadn't grimaced when Isabella had asked him to take Jo outside to entertain her. He had asked her some awkward questions to fill the silence between them, such as why she lived with her grandparents. And she had told him that her mother was dead and that she didn't remember her and that nobody knew who her father was. Gianni had been disconcerted by such honesty, but she had been too naïve to dissemble.

She had told him that she would rather see the library than the garden and he had shown her a shelf with English books and in no time at all she had been curled up in an armchair reading a children's book that had once been his.

'What age are you?' he had finally asked her.

'Eight,' she had told him proudly.

'You're absolutely tiny,' he had remarked.

'I'm not. You're just very tall. My goodness, you can read English as well as Italian,' she had gathered, impressed to death by such an accomplishment.

'If I speak English, I can read it,' Gianni had pointed out. 'My grandmother was English. My mother wanted me to be bilingual. That's why I go to an English school.'

He had attended an elite boarding school, rubbing shoulders with the rich, the titled and the royal. In spite of his mother's illness, he was rarely at Belvedere, and it was the following year before Jo saw him again and in circumstances she would have preferred to forget.

'That poor boy,' she recalled her grandmother saying to her sisters. 'His mother has died and he never got to spend any time with her. He's only home from school and it's too late… She's gone. Isabella said his father was extremely strict about his schooling and wouldn't let him take time out to be with her during her last weeks.'

Jo had been sitting in a tree in the front garden when she saw Gianni in the distance striding down to the lake. Aware that he was grieving, she had not even thought of trying to approach him. She wouldn't have known what to say in such circumstances and it wasn't as though they were friends. There was too big an age gap for that. She had watched as he'd walked into the lake and she had leapt down from the tree, wondering if he knew that there was a very steep drop several yards out, wondering why he wasn't wearing swimwear.

And as he had walked, she had remembered a conversation between her great-aunts that she had overheard, a conversation about her uncle Abraham's death the year before.

'She saw him do it!' Trixie had sobbed. 'How could he do that to his mother? She saw him drown from her bedroom window. She watched him walk into the water and keep on walking until he vanished below the surface. She started running and she was screaming.

'But she was too late. It was all over by the time we got down there.'

At the time, Jo hadn't understood that her uncle had taken his own life, distraught at having lost his family's money in dodgy investments. But she had understood that he had drowned and worry about Gianni had made her break the rule that she was never ever to go near the lake without an adult with her. She had run faster than she had ever run in her life and then she had raced straight into the water to reach Gianni. An accomplished swimmer, she had had no fear.

She had shouted at him just as he'd dipped below the surface but assumed he hadn't heard her. In an effort to help him she had moved in deeper, starting to swim just as her feet had got tangled in the weeds below the surface. As panic had taken hold of her, she'd forgotten everything she had ever learned about how to handle herself in water. She'd struggled, flailing her arms wildly as she'd tried to free her legs and she'd only sunk deeper and faster into the murky depths.

That was all she remembered until she'd

surfaced again, spluttering and gasping on the shore. Gianni's eyes had been wild and desperate above hers, a fierce burning gold as he'd turned her over and urged her to breathe.

So, who had saved whom? she still wondered. It had never been discussed because she had never told anyone the truth of what she had suspected: that Gianni, devastated by his mother's death, had gone into the lake with no plan to come out of it again alive. Certainly, she would have drowned had he not grabbed her and dragged her out of the water to get her breathing again. Ever since then she had given the lake a wide berth, reluctant to revisit those memories.

She had no appetite for her evening meal and her grandmother scolded her, telling her that she was already thin enough. To keep the older woman happy, she agreed to have some soup but, in reality, when Jo was apprehensive all appetite deserted her.

'I suppose you'll offer Gianni the lakeshore land in return,' Liz Hamilton assumed quietly. 'You might as well. Nobody here has fished the lake since your uncle died.'

'I have to offer him something. Our roof

won't go through another winter,' Jo pointed out ruefully.

'The roof on my shop needs attention as well,' Trixie piped up.

'The roof of the house is more important,' Sybil countered. 'And then there's the rewiring. That's next on the list before we get disconnected for failing safety standards.'

'Yes, one thing does lead to another.' Liz sighed heavily. 'The wiring stymied Jo's plans to open a bed and breakfast here. Everything demands money and we don't have any. We only bring in enough cash to pay the weekly bills.'

Her shoulders down-curving, Jo pushed her soup plate away. Sometimes it all got on top of her: the sheer weight of responsibility, the robbing Peter to pay Paul outlook she had to maintain, the need to stretch every penny until it squeaked. Essentially the family had coped until her uncle had lost the family savings and then her grandfather, who had had a good business head on his shoulders, had died. Jo had planned to use her business degree to find a job but supporting Ladymead and her family had had to come first. And she had had some good ideas to bring in an income from the unused buildings in the rear courtyard. Unfortunately, any changes or improvements required to *make* money also *cost* money.

Trixie now had a little shop selling crystals, candles and handicrafts. She was also much in demand for tarot readings locally. Sybil's heart was in the small animal shelter she ran in the barn, but she also sold the organic vegetables grown in the walled garden via their one surviving employee, Maurice, who was as old as the hills, lived in the courtyard and refused to retire.

Duffy flew in and landed on the chair in front of Jo and began to sing the song from a popular musical about money making the world go around.

'You said money, the *fatal* word, and he heard it,' Sybil reproved her big sister.

'It's better than the biblical quotes, although he's amazingly soulful when he starts reciting Shakespeare's sonnets,' Trixie said fondly.

'He's a very well-educated parrot,' Liz Hamilton murmured with quiet pride.

Jo left them to it and went to freshen up, Fairy, a graceful greyhound, gliding upstairs with her. Their Scottie, McTavish, who hated everyone but Jo, was out chasing rabbits, which was just as well when she was planning to visit Belvedere. He had a particular vicious dislike of Gianni, and his housekeeper had had to phone her twice recently to come and retrieve the little animal when McTavish had lain in hopeful wait for Gianni.

She smoothed down her faded blue sundress and sighed, loosening her long hair from its untidy fraying braid and deciding simply to brush it to save time. Gianni was such a stickler for punctuality. She couldn't afford to get off on the wrong foot with him, could she?

Fairy by her side, she climbed into the pickup truck that was the only vehicle left at Ladymead, its usage on a strict schedule to allow all of them a chance to take advantage of the freedom it brought. Gianni had a huge garage full of cars of all descriptions, most of them of the fast, sports variety. Her smile dimmed as she recalled their most significant meeting in recent times.

It had been very awkward. Gianni had attended Ralph's funeral, lingering long enough to offer her his personal condolences on her 'loss'. Ralph Scott had died in a military helicopter crash. He had been a friend, but just about everyone, with the exception of her family, had believed that Jo and Ralph were unofficially engaged. In reality, the engagement had been a story put around by Ralph to save face when he'd discovered that his former fiancée, Jane, was cheating on him with his best friend. Jo had been shocked when Ralph died but she had grieved only over the loss of a dear friend, not over the loss of a man she loved. She would have liked to explain that to Gianni but with so many people standing nearby she hadn't had the opportunity.

Even so, Gianni had tried to offer her comfort in his own unique way, declaring that loving someone only got you hurt, and when she'd queried that statement, he had admitted that he had had his heart broken when he was younger and had learned a useful lesson from the experience. She had been stunned that he should have told her something that personal even though she hadn't agreed with his outlook. Ever since she had wondered who the woman was and what had happened between them.

Suppressing those untimely and inappropriate reflections, Jo parked at the front of the house, crunching over the gravel in her grass-stained canvas sandals to the imposing front entrance. The door opened, Gianni's plump housekeeper, Abigail, bestowing a smile on her before ushering her in.

'Mr Renzetti is in the orangery. It's lovely there at this time of year with the terrace doors wide and the evening sunshine flooding in,' she said, showing Jo through the big echoing hall out to the leafy splendour of the orangery. 'How have you been? I ran into your grandmother yesterday and she said you'd been terribly busy.'

'There's never enough hours in my day,' Jo admitted rather breathlessly as she heard footsteps crossing the tiled floor, strong, sure, like the man himself.

'Jojo,' Gianni purred. 'What are you collecting for this evening?'

He had told her once that Josephine was too much of a mouthful and that Jo made her sound like a boy and he had begun calling her Jojo even though she frowned every time he utilised it.

'C-collecting?' She stammered out the

word, colour rising in her cheeks as she stared at him.

At the worst possible moment, she was remembering that grainy image of him in a suit in that room with that half-naked woman. Her tummy flipped, butterflies breaking free. Her grandmother had told her that Gianni was their neighbour and acquaintance and that it was disrespectful to have that rag of a newspaper in their home when he had been extorted and unaware of the camera. She had been ashamed of herself for devouring every dirty detail. And she was even more ashamed to feel the prickling of her nipples as they tightened and the heat rising between her thighs. But at the end of the day, she was a woman like any other and her body betrayed her in his presence because he *was* that irresistible.

Standing only bare feet away from him, she was shockingly aware of how incredibly handsome he was, how tall, how well built. His beautifully tailored dark pinstriped suit fitted him perfectly and it was designer fashionable, cut to enhance his broad chest and lean muscular thighs. Unaffected by Jo's self-consciousness, Fairy located a rug, turned three times and settled down happily for a snooze.

'For charity. When you visit you're always collecting for something but you don't usually go for the formality of making an appointment,' Gianni clarified lazily, studying her with veiled eyes, the stirring sexual pulse at his groin all too familiar and fiercely resisted.

Josephine Hamilton was exquisite. There was no other word. The pretty child had grown into an incredibly beautiful woman with a mane of golden hair, sapphire-blue eyes, a delicate little nose and a luscious pink mouth. She was a slender five feet four or so with the grace of a ballet dancer and sometimes when he saw her, she could still take his breath away. A member of the church choir, she had been among the carol singers that had called at Belvedere the previous Christmas, her lovely face the only one he'd noticed in the crowd, her jewelled eyes shining, golden hair rumpled and, for once, she had been smiling at him.

Gianni laughed at her blank look. 'You were collecting for the homeless last time you were here, and you did very well out of my dinner guests. Your speech could have wrung water from a stone.'

Jo coloured again. 'Yes, they were very generous, but I wouldn't have called in had I known that you were entertaining.'

'Come and sit down,' he suggested as his housekeeper bustled in with a tray of coffee and cakes.

'Nothing for me,' Jo said tightly, both nervous and embarrassed as she sank down into a basketwork cushioned chair.

'You usually eat like a horse,' Gianni remarked in surprise. 'What's wrong? You seem very tense.'

Jo stiffened. 'You're treating me like a welcome visitor and that doesn't feel right when I've come to ask you for a loan,' she confided uncomfortably.

It was so Jojo to just blurt it out like that and he was wryly amused. 'I'm not a bank,' he said quietly.

'The banks said no.'

Gianni concealed his amusement with difficulty. 'You really shouldn't be telling me that in advance.'

Jo lifted her chin. 'I'm not stupid. I know you would check that out.'

'What do you need the loan for? *The money pit?*'

Jojo compressed her lips, offended by that label being attached to her home. 'The roof is in a bad way and the wiring is causing problems. I want to set up a bed and breakfast and the regulations are extremely strict.'

Gianni schooled his shrewd gaze. His father had been obsessed with acquiring Ladymead and ridding the neighbourhood of the eccentric Hamiltons and the folksy business operations they had cobbled together to stay afloat. Officially, Gianni had owned Belvedere since he was thirteen and the presence of a Tudor dump on the other side of the screening wall his parent had erected bothered him not at all.

'Of course, I'm not expecting you to help out of the goodness of your heart.'

'Well, you know I have none of that,' Gianni inserted drily.

'You didn't report McTavish for biting you,' Jo reminded him in disagreement.

'You'd never have forgiven me.'

'I know you don't like long-winded speeches, so I'll get straight to the point. We're willing to sell the lakeshore land to you.'

Gianni gritted his teeth and groaned. How did he tell her that when the Hamiltons eventually went bust he would buy Ladymead on the cheap, close the shops and install tenants? It was an historic building, as he had reminded his father, and it couldn't be demolished. But what exasperated him the most was Jo's admission that she was planning a bed and breakfast operation.

'How on earth could you cope with guests in the house? You're already run ragged trying to keep the place going,' Gianni demanded impatiently. 'You would have to renovate the entire house and you would need staff. Trixie would need to stop worshipping at her shrine to nature in the back garden. Sybil would have to stop taking in every stray animal that comes along. Your grandmother, who isn't getting any younger, would never get out of the kitchen. It's not a viable proposition.'

'I didn't ask for *your* opinion,' Jo told him tartly.

Gianni sprang up restively. 'Too bad... you're getting it. It's a totally impractical ambition.'

'And you just expect me to accept your

judgement on that score, do you?' Jo slung back at him angrily.

'I do,' Gianni delivered succinctly. 'I know you have a business degree, but you've not used it or been out in the world. You don't have the experience to—'

'If being out in the world means shagging some trollop in a questionable club and making sleazy headlines, then I don't think I want to be *out* in the world as you put it!' Her face flushed, her hands knotted into fists, her sapphire eyes alight with fury, Jo stared him down in challenge.

CHAPTER TWO

GIANNI FROZE, UNPREPARED FOR that level of anger and vitriol from her lips because Josephine Hamilton was known far and wide as a very kind woman with endless compassion, a woman who never put a foot wrong. And she had just hit a spectacular own goal. His lean, darkly handsome features were taut but his glittering dark-as-night eyes took on an arrested expression as he stared back at her rigid figure because all of a sudden, he was seeing possibilities he had never dreamt he might consider. She had a backbone of steel and an astonishing streak of honesty, regardless of the circumstances, and he respected those traits.

In that same timeless moment, Jo turned pale as death, overpowered with regret for those fiery, merciless words. Such an attack had been beneath her and a low blow when it came to such a sensitive subject. Particularly when he had welcomed her warmly into his home. Since when had she stood in judgement over others?

'Gianni…' she said stiltedly. 'I am really sorry. That was cruel, unkind, and derogatory. I don't know what came over me…or maybe I do. The past few weeks…all the bank visits and getting shot down in flames, trying to pretend everything was normal for my grandmother to keep her calm. I'm afraid the stress got to me and that I took it out on you. But that's not an excuse.'

'No, it's not,' Gianni agreed very quietly. 'And a highly inadvisable approach for someone in need of a loan. But because you were honest, I will be equally frank. Repossession or bankruptcy was always on the cards for you and Ladymead because you lack the income to support living in such a house. I planned to pick up Ladymead when you were forced to leave it. It's not a burning ambition for me as it was for my father, but there is no advantage to me in helping you or your family to remain there.'

'I kind of guessed that,' she muttered un-

evenly, still pale as milk and trembling a little
from the shock of losing her temper to such
an extent and the struggle it was not to tell
him things that he wouldn't want to hear.

Such as the fact that he was worth so much
more than those sleazy headlines. He had succumbed to the temptation of some slutty scam
artist, but he could do so much better and
would be so much happier if only he would
put value on something less ephemeral than
a cheap sexual thrill. It infuriated her that
he was so short-sighted, so set against falling in love, so determined to reduce relationships between men and women to the lowest
common denominator. And it shamed her
that, when she had first seen that photo, she
had been jealous that it wasn't *her* with him.
Naturally, an alternative imaginary version
of her, a woman sexually confident enough
to tease him in a raunchy corset. And how
weird and unforgivable was that when she
had thrown his miscalculation in his teeth
like a challenge?

How much worse was it that instead of con-
centrating on his refusal to loan her family
money, she was knee deep and wallowing

in a personal reaction to Gianni that had no place between them?

'I'll leave now,' she muttered, calling Fairy from her slumber, eager to be gone and yet devastated that he had refused to help her family. Somehow, inexplicably, even though she had known that a positive answer would have gone against his essentially predatory nature, she had still contrived to hope for a different response.

'Join me for dinner at La Vie en Rose tomorrow evening. I'll pick you up at eight,' Gianni told her, rather than *asked* her. 'I may have a solution for you that also benefits me but I want a day to think the concept over. And, no, don't shoot yourself in the foot by voicing another knee-jerk refusal to my invitation!'

Flustered by that unexpected assurance and the invitation, Jo snatched in a ragged breath and nodded her head. Dinner with Gianni? No, don't think about that, she urged herself irritably. Think about what kind of solution to her family's financial problems could possibly offer benefit to a filthy rich Renzetti, blessed in every way. Her mind was a complete blank. But of course he wasn't blessed in *every* way, she reminded herself ruefully. Being rich didn't protect Gianni from having problems, not least the scandal that he had unleashed with his uninhibited sexual appetite.

He owned the very exclusive French restaurant in the village. Nobody in Jo's family had ever dined there because it was Michelin-starred and extremely expensive. Well, no doubt if she could get over her nervous tummy, she would at least enjoy a rare treat, she told herself soothingly as she packed Fairy back into the pickup truck.

Gianni strode through to the drawing room and poured himself a brandy while watching Jojo drive off in her battered, noisy vehicle. He had not seriously considered the possibility of taking his father's advice and getting married until he found himself involuntarily picturing Jojo in the role. Jojo was a perfect fit for his blueprint. She had impeccable credentials. Charitable work, church work, loyal to her family, former fiancée of a decorated soldier. Her reputation was so clean it shone like a halo next to his own.

Gianni had few illusions about himself. He

knew that he was brilliant in business. He also knew that he was ruthless, occasionally callous, selfish and quick-tempered, not to mention sporadically impulsive. And right at this very moment, a foolish and fleeting sexual impulse was threatening to destroy his career and everything he had worked so hard to achieve. Nothing less than that threat would have induced him to consider marriage to *any* woman.

Jojo, however, was in a class of her own. For a start, Gianni found her very attractive and she had all the allure of being the only woman who had ever said no to him. He had wanted her for several years and had resolutely suppressed that desire. On two occasions when the desire had overpowered his scruples, he had invited her out to dinner. Ironically, he had felt weirdly relieved when she had turned him down. After all, prior to his current crisis, what could he have offered her? She would have wanted meaningful, and he would have wanted a one-night stand. He was well aware of his limitations. Keeping his distance had been the kindest thing he could do for both of them.

Marriage held little attraction for him. His

parents had been miserable together even before cancer first afflicted his mother. They had had separate bedrooms and his father had kept a mistress and nothing could have hidden the truth that his parents had barely a thought in common. Even raising their only child had been a cause of disagreement between them, his father insisting that his mother was too soft with him, his mother refusing to forgive his father for sending Gianni to boarding school. Nobody was more aware than Gianni that marriage could be a stony road paved with obstacles and bitterness. Yet he was equally aware that his seemingly cold father had grieved deeply after his wife's death and he had never understood that conundrum. Jojo was of a different ilk, Gianni reasoned. There was nothing cold, hard or bitter about her. She would, undoubtedly, endeavour to improve him but he decided that he could live with that just as he was likely to have to live with generous doses of the crazy parrot, the nutty family and the homicidal McTavish. In return, she would take care of his homes, act as his hostess and nag him into attending church more often. But in spite of the drawbacks he foresaw, he also believed she was a catch and a top-quality one.

Unaware of the sterling talents being awarded to her, Jo returned to her family and explained only that Gianni would give her an answer over dinner the following evening.

'He's trying to get his pound of flesh,' Sybil opined darkly. 'He's finally getting you out to dinner. Make sure you don't end up on the dessert menu, Jo!'

'It's a business proposition. He probably wants to check everything out first,' her grandmother reproved her sister. 'He would have to consult his solicitor and estate manager as well.'

'Have you seen the way Gianni Renzetti looks at Jo?' Sybil scoffed. 'Like she's a juicy rabbit and he's a fox!'

'Are you trying to put Jo off dining with him?' Trixie asked, glancing at her great-niece's burning cheeks. 'I'm quite sure he will be able to restrain himself for one meal.'

'What on earth are you going to wear?' Sybil pressed.

'The dress I wore to Ralph's regimental dinner.'

'Oh, yes, that's very pretty on you, and I'll do your make-up and hair,' Sybil announced with pleasure.

'So although you don't think he can be trusted, you're happy to doll her up like a human sacrifice?' Trixie sniffed disapprovingly.

'Will you stop worrying? I can look after myself,' Jo declared with quiet confidence, and she left her relatives to do a stint in Trixie's shop so that her great-aunt could enjoy a longer tea break.

That same confidence had dwindled a good deal by the time Gianni drew up at Ladymead in a very snazzy sportscar. Jo had gone for a more natural look than Sybil favoured, reluctant to appear as though she had made a huge effort to impress him. In any case it would be a wasted effort, she reflected, considering the beauties Gianni was regularly seen with. Even at her best, she could not compete with a supermodel.

Watching her climb ineptly into the low-slung car, her full skirt flipping up, Gianni, treated to a glimpse of slender thigh and very shapely legs, was entranced, arousal humming through him in a persistent pulse that would not be stilled. The subtle light scent of something flowery assailed him.

'Have you eaten here before?' he asked as he parked the car.

'No. It's a little pricey for us,' Jo said lightly. 'I heard that there's a waiting list for a table.'

'It's proved immensely popular. Wait,' he urged as she moved to open the passenger door.

He opened the door for her and reached down a lean brown hand to help her out of the car, his hand dropping lightly to her waist to guide her onto the pavement, her spine prickling with a powerful awareness of his touch and proximity.

'Is this the treatment all your women receive?' Jo joked as she smoothed down her skirts and preceded him into the restaurant.

'No. You're in a class of your own.'

Aside from hovering staff, there wasn't a single other diner. Jo lifted a brow and settled down into the private booth. The lights were low, a candle burned and fresh flowers adorned the table. 'Gosh, this feels like a *real* date,' she quipped.

'It must be. You put lip gloss on,' Gianni fielded silkily.

'You should feel short-changed. Sybil tried to get me into false lashes and something she called a smoky eye,' she revealed, dark blue eyes wide with amusement.

'You don't need them. I like the restrained, natural look.'

Says the man seduced by a corset and a thong, Jo thought wryly, but at least she didn't make the mistake of saying it out loud.

'Why's it so quiet in here?'

'The restaurant was fully booked but I wanted privacy for what I have to say to you,' Gianni explained levelly. 'Next week the diners we displaced will enjoy their meal at my expense.'

As the wine arrived, along with a selection of tiny tasters and plates, Jo swallowed hard and pinched her thigh to keep herself alert. She knew that she had to stay on top form to deal with Gianni.

'What on earth do you need privacy for?' she asked bluntly, rebelling against the insidious intimacy of their setting.

'Will you listen to my proposition without interrupting me?'

'I'll try.' Jo lifted her wine glass, suddenly all of a quiver with nerves.

'The consequences of the scandal I caused mean that I require a wife,' Gianni told her wryly. 'I need to be seen to be settling down to retain my position as CEO of Renzetti Inc, otherwise I've been warned that I'll be voted out at the end of the month. You strike me as perfect wife material.'

Jo gulped but she couldn't find her voice to interrupt. She was stunned by that assurance and flattered as well, although the part of her that felt gratified was feeling that way very much against her will. Her attention clung to the mesmeric tawny golden glow of his black-fringed eyes in the candlelight, the shadows cast below his slanting cheekbones and the lush pink of his full lower lip.

'I won't *loan* you the money you need, *cara*. I'm telling you that upfront,' Gianni spelt out with perfect diction as he helpfully divided up the tasters on the platter and served her. 'What would be the point of giving you a loan that you couldn't afford to repay?'

She drank down her wine to ease her dry

throat and inside her chest her heart thumped at a fast drumbeat. He was giving it all to her, piece by piece, breaking the situation down into what he probably saw as manageable chunks. Didn't he realise that labelling her as 'perfect wife material' simply blew a giant hole in her concentration? The idea of marrying Gianni Renzetti struck her as so incredible that she was wondering if she had somehow misunderstood him at some point during that speech.

'You're in so much debt that even the sale of the lakeshore land wouldn't turn the situation around,' Gianni told her succinctly. 'I suspect that your bank must be close to considering foreclosure.'

Jo only just contrived to suppress a shudder, but their bank had given her the same impression when she had had the temerity to ask for a new loan. Her family's financial situation was dire. Insufficient money coming in and too many bills had sent the overdraft climbing the previous winter and she heaved a sigh.

'I feel like such a failure,' she muttered tightly.

'You're not a failure. Previous generations

of your family neglected the property. That house has been in decline for many years and a full-scale restoration is probably required now. Are you struggling to hang onto the house for your grandmother's benefit?'

Jo grimaced and shook her head. 'No. I'm more selfish. Ladymead has been in the family for hundreds of years. I don't want to be the one to lose it. I know once it's gone, it's gone for ever. I also know that even though it's in poor condition I love every historic nook and cranny in that building,' she confessed ruefully. 'My earliest memories are of Grandad taking me round Ladymead and sharing his recollections of *his* childhood.'

Gianni studied her lovely face in the low light, the plush peach curve of her lower lip as she worried at it with the edge of her teeth, and an almost blinding surge of lust tightened every muscle in his long lean body. He topped up her wine and rested back in his seat, suppressing that arousal with all his strength.

'My next question has to be are you *willing* to marry me to keep Ladymead in your family?' he asked levelly. 'If you marry me I will finance the restoration of the house. I

will cover every necessary expense and ensure your family's security and comfort.'

Jo blinked rapidly and began to eat in haste,
needing that simple act to ground herself
again. What Gianni was offering was the ful-
filment of her wildest dreams. She would be
able to stop worrying and give up trying to
work every hour of the day while trying to
dream up new ways to make or save money.
In addition, her family would be safe and secure and freed from the same anxiety.

'Gianni…you haven't thought this through.'

'On the contrary, I've thought very deeply
about it.'

'Why me?' she demanded helplessly. 'I
mean, there must be so many women who
would be eager to marry you.'

'I need your respectability and you need
my money, but you're not a gold-digger. That
is an important distinction for me,' he admitted as the main course was brought to their
table.

'What sort of marriage are you talking
about?' Jo enquired uncertainly.

Gianni frowned, shapely ebony brows rising enquiringly as if she had asked an unexpected question. 'A normal marriage.'

'Normal?' Jo questioned, her incredulity obvious, her eyes wide. 'Like share-a-bed, have-children normal?'

'What else?'

Jo flushed. 'We could *fake* it…being married, I mean, and just do the surface show for the sake of appearances. Surely that would gain you just as much?'

'I don't do fake, *cara*,' Gianni murmured softly. 'I'm not keen to try celibacy and the alternative is to play away and take the chance of being exposed as an adulterer. In the current moral climate in which I work I'm not prepared to run that risk…'

Jo cut into her tender steak with determination. 'I understand…' she conceded reluctantly. 'I was only trying to suggest a more workable version of what you proposed.'

'A promise to keep my hands off you would—inevitably—be broken,' Gianni told her frankly. 'I've been attracted to you for a long time. I have to be truthful on that score. I wouldn't be asking you to marry me if I didn't find you attractive. *Dio mio*, I assume that if we have reached the stage of discussing sex, you're thinking about it…'

'Of course, I'm thinking about it,' Jo protested in a guilty, stifled undertone. 'My family means everything to me, and we've all been working really hard to keep things afloat and yet, we're still sliding down the slippery slope of debt at speed. Then you come along like some knight on a white charger…'

Gianni raised a lean brown hand at that point to silence her. 'No. I'll never be your knight on a white charger. I haven't been in a relationship for a long time and I've no doubt that I'll be challenging to live with. But I assure you that I will look after you and your family to the best of my ability.'

It was like a lifebelt being thrown to Jo just when she felt as though she were on the very brink of drowning. She had had a mad crush on Gianni when she was a teenager but half the girls at school had been equally keen to see Gianni Renzetti as a pin-up. That glimpses of him were rare had merely added to his mystique. Seen around the village only at weekends and holidays, Gianni, clad in designer jeans and driving a flash car, had been the perfect adolescent fantasy figure.

'You're staring…' Gianni breathed. 'What's going through your mind?'

'You don't want to know.' Jo shook her head as though to clear it and frowned at him as she pushed away her plate, ashamed that she could be allowing teenaged fantasies to influence her when all such nonsense was long since dead and buried. 'I just can't believe that you're asking me to marry you.'

'Get with the programme, *cara*,' he urged, and that faint hint of impatience only gave his slight accent a smoky edge, an effect which was underscored by the gentle stroke of his forefinger across the back of her hand. 'We're way beyond that stage. We're negotiating.'

'Are we?' Jo sighed. 'You have unlimited confidence, Gianni.'

'And secretly, you like that about me. If we set the parameters now there'll be no room for misunderstandings,' he asserted with remarkable optimism.

'I haven't said that I accept yet,' Jo protested in dismay. 'I need tomorrow to think about stuff. But misunderstandings will occur whatever we discuss beforehand. Perhaps what we really need is a time-limited agreement.'

His ebony brows drew together in a gathering frown as the dessert trolley arrived. 'What sort of limit?'

Jo turned aside to order her dessert. 'Six months?' she suggested.

'Why bother getting married in the first place?' Gianni asked drily. 'It's nowhere near long enough and it wouldn't fool anyone into believing I was settling down.'

'A year?'

In response, Gianni simply frowned and shook his head in immediate dismissal.

He said that he disliked sweet things and had ordered coffee, which she knew for a fact he drank with a ridiculous amount of sugar in it. As in other fields, Gianni could be wildly unpredictable. Hadn't she simply assumed that he would leap at the offer of a six-month marital stretch?

'What if there's a child to be considered?' Gianni asked.

'That's why it might be wiser to leave the possibility of children out of the arrangement,' Jo proposed, stifling a pang of disappointment at that prospect even if it was the more sensible option.

Gianni dealt her a frowning look of reproof. 'If we're planning to play house, we should do it properly. I don't only partially commit to a new project. If we're doing this, I want the whole shebang.'

Jo swallowed slowly and nodded. *The whole shebang.* A normal marriage, Gianni as a husband, Gianni in the same bed most nights. She burned as a surge of fantasy-induced heat washed through the most sensitive places in her body. There was no use pretending to herself that she wasn't curious about what *that* would be like. Her skin warmed. She couldn't imagine being in bed with Gianni but she had had one or two totally wanton fantasies about him over the years. And yet tonight was the very first time he had truly touched her. She didn't count that time he had saved her from drowning in the lake as a child.

Gianni wasn't a touchy-feely type of guy and he was circumspect about not touching a woman unnecessarily. That was why every physical touch he had utilised since picking her up for dinner had very clearly underlined the change he now saw in their relationship. A tiny little shiver snaked through her taut frame. She liked that change, that revealing shift away from casual friendship. But he wasn't 'courting' her, wasn't offering her a wedding ring on the usual terms, she reminded herself irritably. He had utilised the word *normal*, but two people who were not in love opting to marry was *not* normal, in her view, particularly when one of them was endeavouring to bury a scandal by putting on a public front of embracing respectability.

'Let's go,' Gianni intoned a few minutes later when she had finished dessert. 'Unless you want coffee as well.'

'No, I don't drink coffee this late,' Jo muttered, torn in two by the conflicting reactions assailing her.

Without Gianni, her family would forfeit Ladymead and any security, for once the debts were settled, there would be little, if anything, left to support another life elsewhere. With Gianni on board, those debts and the worry caused by them would disappear.

But what would it cost her personally to marry a man she didn't love? A man who was very unlikely ever to love her? That was the big question…

CHAPTER THREE

'WHAT ARE YOU agonising about?' Gianni prompted as he ignited the car engine.

'I'm not agonising about anything,' Jo lied.

In reality, Jo was glancing back with a near wince at the couple of colourless forgettable romances she had had over the years. She didn't even count Ralph, who had asked her to marry him purely as a face-saving move. He had never been more than a friend. Sadly, she had only ever met one man who inspired anything more than liking in her and that felt like a personal failure. She had told herself off for being too choosy, too critical, particularly when she had always been conscious that she wanted a long-term relationship and children in her future.

And yet here she was, twenty-four years old and still a virgin and the only man she had ever really, *really* fancied was Gianni Renzetti. What did that say about her? That she was an unrealistic dreamer? Gianni had always seemed totally unobtainable. But now he had shocked her with a proposition she could never have foreseen, and the sensible side of her brain was in conflict with the idealistic side.

'About marrying me?' Gianni guided the powerful car smoothly into the rough, pot-holed lane that led to her family home and slowed down to a snail's pace. 'If the marriage didn't work out, if we were miserable a few years down the road, we could separate, and it wouldn't be the end of the world. Unfortunately, you don't like risks, *cara*, and I accept that you must see me as a high-risk venture.'

'Where do you get the idea that I don't like risks?' Jo demanded curtly, annoyed by the confidence with which he spoke.

'You choose the safe, sensible path most of the time. You did your business degree and you brought it home and let your family bury you alive in *their* problems. You don't seem to have a single streak of ruthlessness. If you had, you would have walked away and made your own life.'

'My family and my home *are* my life. I had a poor start as a baby but my family loved me enough to overlook those beginnings and they gave me a very happy childhood,' Jo argued vehemently.

Jo was troubled just thinking about what she might have been like without the family who had raised her and given her so much love. She didn't remember her mother and knew little about her but she knew that her mother had wanted to share her child with her family. And truly, there was nothing Jo wouldn't do for that same family, who had given her so much, and she knew that she owed every ounce of her strength and self-respect to the way she had been brought up.

Gianni parked the car. 'You can keep your family close if you marry me,' he murmured in silken addition.

Jo shot him a furious glance. 'I *know*! Is there anything you won't use to get your own way?'

'Probably extraordinarily little,' Gianni breathed, his wide mobile mouth taking on a cynical twist. 'You should probably ask me about the scandal.'

In receipt of that unexpected piece of advice,

Jo turned red with mortification and, reaching for the door handle, opened the door to clamber out in haste. 'It's none of my business.'

Gianni sprang out of the driver's seat and stalked round the low-slung bonnet of the car like a man bracing himself. 'I asked you to marry me. You have a right to know the facts. The woman concerned was a model, not someone I knew whom I could trust. We dined together in a private room at the club. I had no suspicion that I was being set up as, to be frank, I had utilised a private room in that way before. Sex without even leaving the building...it was convenient for both me and the women concerned.'

Jo's face felt so hot it felt as though it were on fire. Heaven forbid, she thought helplessly, that any man would ever view the sharing of her body as a mere convenience.

'I left myself open to extortion. That kind of behaviour in my position was reckless. I didn't think. I didn't pause to consider what I was doing or where I was. I just took what was on offer for all the usual dumb male reasons.'

'Oh, dear,' Jo mumbled uncomfortably.

An involuntary laugh of appreciation escaped Gianni. 'I was a complete idiot,' he admitted, closing long fingers round her narrow wrist to ease her closer.

'No arguments from this corner.' Her mouth ran dry as she looked up at him in the moonlight.

He looked breathtakingly handsome, a powerful intensity etched in his lean, hard features and in the narrowed set of his stunning dark golden eyes. He ran a finger slowly across her cheekbone and her gaze widened, her breathing fracturing as he eased her back against the bonnet of the car. 'I want to kiss you.'

'Go ahead,' she heard herself mumble without hesitation because having got this close to Gianni she had no intention of denying herself that experience. Unsteady on her feet, nervous as a cat on hot bricks, she trembled when he brought her into full contact with his lean, powerful body. His arms closed round her, lifting her up to him as he circled her closed lips with his, plucking at the lower with his teeth, sending a shard of sharp craving arrowing down into her belly. His mouth travelled everywhere but where she wanted, teasing and dancing across her cheek before grazing down the soft slope of her neck and making her shudder in reaction and arch into his heat and strength.

'Don't do that. I'm on an incredibly short fuse,' Gianni growled, one hand suddenly splaying across the rounded curve of her bottom and pressing her into the cradle of his thighs, acquainting her with the hot, hard thrust of the erection shaped by the fine material of his tailored trousers.

Her tummy flipped, warmth and moisture gathering between her thighs as he finally found her mouth and took it with raw hunger.

The power of that smouldering kiss shot through her like an electric shock and her arms wrapped around him, hanging onto him to ensure she stayed upright, fingertips curling into the black hair at his nape. Her body was going haywire, her temperature soaring. His tongue stroked hers and the fierce pulse of desire clenched tight at the heart of her. In turmoil under that racing onslaught of sensation, Jo pulled back.

Gianni closed his hand over hers to prevent her from moving away. 'Are you going to take me indoors to speak to your family? Or are you planning to run away?'

Some inner strength powered Jo into raising her head high even though she was still quaking inside herself from the force of the reaction she was containing. 'Neither. I will deal with my family alone when I've reached a decision.'

'Then give me a decision over breakfast tomorrow at Belvedere. Eight. If we're going to do this, we need to move quickly,' Gianni murmured softly.

Jo had forgotten about the time constraints, and she ground her teeth together. She wanted to hold him at a distance because of the way he had made her feel in his arms and breakfast was only a matter of hours away, not long enough in which to recover her equilibrium and make the most major decision of her life to date.

'*Eight?*' she gasped.

'I'm pushing the time back for your benefit. I usually eat at six.'

'Even on a Sunday?'

'At least you won't miss church,' Gianni pointed out, sliding back into his car with the feral grace of a prowling panther.

Jo discovered that she was still holding her breath as she walked into the house, feeling as though she had gone through several rounds with a top prizefighter, exhausted and yet excited, challenged and yet exhilarated, dazed yet with her mind still racing. Her heart was still pounding inside her, her legs felt weak and wobbly.

Sybil cornered her in the hall. *'Well?'*

Jo smothered a fake yawn. 'We're meeting at eight for breakfast before we make a final decision.'

'We?'

Jo leant closer. 'Can you keep a secret?' She had to tell someone, and she knew that she could trust Sybil. 'He's asked me to marry him and in return he will take care of everything here.'

'I suppose you practically bit his hand off for an offer that good…' Sybil laughed at Jo's shock at that frank estimation. 'You've always wanted him, Jo. This is not exactly coming out of left field, is it? He does need to rehab his image…but are you willing to risk getting hurt?'

Shifting from surprise to acceptance at her great-aunt's shrewd reading of her predicament, Jo smiled. 'Yes. Probably because I don't think I can resist his proposal. If I said no, I'd always wonder if I'd made a mistake and I'm not sure I could bear seeing him marry someone else when it could have been me.'

'Do what's right for *you*,' Sybil urged, giving her an affectionate hug. 'I won't offer you any advice, but do appreciate that I can get a proper job and so can Trixie and we can find somewhere to live. We're far from helpless. I only worry about your grandmother.'

Jo went to bed and lay awake. Her whole body was buzzing with nervous energy.

Gianni couldn't sleep either. He was thinking about getting married and torn between lust and panic at what having a wife would be like. Jojo had standards, *serious* standards. There would be no grey areas with Jojo, no looking the other way. He didn't want to be the kind of husband his father had been: lying and cheating behind his wife's back. He needed to be honest with Jo, however, frank about the reality that he couldn't offer her love. He understood Jo well enough to know that she wouldn't be happy to hear that truth. They would *both* have to make compromises, he acknowledged.

On the lighter side, Jo would turn Belvedere

into a home, something it had not been since
the death of his mother, he mused thoughtfully. Furthermore, it was boredom with the
women he met that had plunged him into that
shabby encounter at the nightclub. Jo was not
boring. She made intelligent conversation and
could be very amusing and there was something about her, something he couldn't define,
that turned him on so hard and fast it should
have been scary. But it was exciting and it had
been a very long time since anything outside
business had truly excited Gianni.

Jo got up early and put on a light skirt and
casual white top, pushing her bare feet into
sandals. She decided to walk over to Belvedere and left Fairy behind slumbering in the
kitchen. McTavish caught up with her on her
walk and she told him to go home repeatedly
while he capered around her in mad excitement at the pheasant he had scared into flight.

'You're not allowed at Gianni's house. You
disgraced yourself,' she reminded him and
she left him whining on the front doorstep
of the mansion.

Abigail led her through the hall. 'Mr Renzetti fancied something less formal than the

dining room, so he had us set up a table on the terrace. I don't know what's got into him,' she whispered. 'He's never eaten breakfast here *outdoors*.'

'It's a beautiful morning,' Jo said soothingly.

She strolled out through the leafy orangery to the terrace and there it was, a table set with all the formality of an Edwardian dining room in the open air. Of course, the housekeeper knew no other way of doing things because Gianni's mother had preferred the pomp and ceremony and Gianni had probably never even bothered to say that he wasn't quite as enamoured about that kind of superficial show. That was assuming that Gianni had even noticed and she was not sure he would or why he had made such a choice. He had about as much interest in how his home ran as she had in high finance.

'Jojo…' Gianni sprang upright, a lean, powerful figure dressed in chinos and a dark green tee. Even casually clad, he looked amazing, his black cropped hair gleaming in the sunshine, heavily lashed dark golden eyes intent as he smiled at her.

'I don't think I've seen you out of a suit

since you were a teenager,' Jo commented, butterflies flying free in her tummy. She was trying not to reel from the charisma of that smile and the knowledge that if she went ahead, she would always be stressing just a little about the worry of having such a very good-looking husband.

'I work at home on Sundays.'

'That'll have to stop. I'm a firm believer in Sunday being a day of rest,' Jo murmured quietly.

Gianni's stunning eyes flashed pure gold and stared into hers with the piercing potency of a laser scalpel. 'Does that *mean...*?'

Abigail bustled about fetching plates, pouring tea and coffee, setting out toast and a basket of *pains au chocolat* that would usually have made Jo's hand reach straight out because they were a favourite of hers.

Jo angled up her delicate chin, sapphire-blue eyes schooled to a tranquil expression, her calm only a surface show when deep down inside she was quaking at the far-reaching effects of the decision she had made. 'I suppose it must. However, there would be conditions.'

His strong jawline clenched. 'Not a fan of

that word, *cara*. I don't like limits and conditions outside the business world.'

The housekeeper finally retreated and left them alone. Jo began sipping her tea with the same air of composure. Only the realisation that her hand was trembling made her set down the cup with a slightly jarring snap of china meeting china. She didn't want Gianni to guess how shaken she was by her own daring choice. She had to be strong with Gianni. If she weren't, he was one of those fiery passionate personalities who would walk all over her. He *had* to respect that she would have demands to make too.

'The first condition is that I won't be sharing a bed with you until *I* feel comfortable with that idea.'

'Even though we'll be married?'

'We haven't even dated. I know you as a neighbour, a casual acquaintance. I will be happy to share a bed with you when we're in a proper relationship as a couple, but not before that,' Jo extended.

The minute Gianni had registered that she was agreeing to marry him he had planned to ask her to stay that very night with him.

An annoyance that came from the strangest sense of hurt rejection rippled through his lean, powerful frame and he suppressed the reaction, knowing that he only wanted Jo to be with him when *she* felt right about the idea. Anything less was inconceivable to him. 'So, I will also be on trial as a husband?'

'That's not how I see it. I view it as a reasonable request.'

'I can understand your feelings,' Gianni responded.

Jo succumbed to a crispy soft *pain au chocolat* and tore off a piece of flaky pastry. She felt naïve for not having foreseen that that condition of hers would be challenging for him to accept.

Gianni raked long brown fingers through his luxuriant black hair and paced to the edge of the terrace, tension in the lines of his powerful physique, his broad shoulders squared, his long legs braced apart. Just as suddenly he swung back to her. 'And you think that this would get our marriage off to a good start?' he queried in a calm tone, making it clear that it was a genuine question, not a scornful one.

Jo nodded, relief flowing through her in a

heady wave that made her feel slightly dizzy.
'I do.'

'Then so it will be. I accept your terms,'
Gianni conceded levelly. 'I don't do relationships with women, *cara*. You have to tell me
what you want and need and, as you have
just seen, I'm not always fast on the uptake.'

'But you *did* have a relationship while you
were at university,' Jo reminded him.

Gianni froze in front of her, eyes narrowing, spectacular cheekbones taut, his stubborn
mouth compressing. 'I only told you *that* because I was trying to express sympathy for
your loss. It was unwise of me and I would
like you to forget that confidence. It is not a
topic I care to revisit.'

Jo turned pale at that chilling little speech.
It definitely wasn't the optimum moment to
tell him that Ralph Scott had not been her
fiancé or the love of her life, since evidently
Gianni regretted telling her even as little as
he had about his past relationship. She felt
snubbed and hurt and embarrassed all at the
same time.

'Maybe I should go home…' she began
awkwardly, just as a warning growl sounded
from the depths of the shrubbery closest to

Gianni. It was a welcome interruption and she was instantly upright to stalk over there and say angrily. 'McTavish…go home, *right now*!'

'I was expecting him,' Gianni confessed. 'He follows you everywhere.'

He returned to the table and lifted a steel dome on the trolley to reveal a massive meaty bone. He picked it up with a wince of distaste and as the terrier erupted from the shrubbery he dropped it on the grass. McTavish screeched to a halt and sniffed the bone with the enthusiasm of a dog whose every Christmas had come at once. He lost all interest in Gianni and concentrated on trying to drag the giant bone away.

'My goodness…' Jo whispered.

'He'd much rather chew on that than my leg,' Gianni said drily. 'Sit down, *cara*. I have something to give you.'

Her smooth brow pleating, Jo dropped back down into her seat.

Gianni extended his hand, palm upright. An extraordinarily elaborate jewelled ring lay in the centre of it. 'Your engagement ring. If you don't like it, I'll get you something more contemporary. It's from my mother's collection of medieval jewellery and the sapphires and diamonds are of the highest quality. It once belonged to an Italian *duchessa*, but if you want more information on its background, you'll have to look up my mother's catalogues for yourself.'

An engagement ring? No, she hadn't been expecting that, but she supposed that it tied in with his desire for them to look and behave like a normal couple. She stared down at the rich blue sapphires and the glittering diamonds in wonder. 'It's absolutely gorgeous,' she muttered weakly, still in shock at the gesture.

More relaxed now, Gianni strode round the table and lifted it from her again to slide it onto her finger. 'It'll need resizing, I'm sure... *Dio mio*, you have tiny fingers.' As the ring settled into place as though it had been made for her, Gianni smiled down at her. 'Now, isn't that a good omen? While you eat your breakfast you can tell me about your other conditions.'

Jo was reluctant to speak up after the reaction her first condition had drawn from him. 'Er...well, maybe this is not the right time.'

'It is the *only* time,' Gianni sliced in smoothly.

Jo swallowed hard. 'Well...er, fidelity.'

Gianni tossed her a withering glance.

'Don't even say it. I'm not going to cheat on you. My father had other women throughout his marriage. I will not be following in his footsteps. What else?'

'You have to make an effort not to work all the time.'

'Monday through Friday, I will make no promises, but weekends and holidays I will be entirely yours,' Gianni asserted with characteristic certainty.

Jo chanced a sip of tea and a sliver of her pastry but she was strung too high on nerves to swallow easily. Her mind had fallen on that 'entirely yours' phrase like a vulture and refused to move beyond that level.

Gianni sank down on the seat beside hers and reached for a piece of pastry and held it up to her mouth with amusement. 'You have to eat, Jojo…you barely ate last night and this morning you're starving yourself again. You need your strength,' he told her softly. 'How else can you hope to hold me at bay on our honeymoon? I've got skills at seduction like you wouldn't believe.'

Jo almost choked on that piece of pastry as a laugh escaped her, unexpected happiness bubbling up through her. 'Promises, promises.'

'I can't give you love but I do know what women want and I believe I can make you happy,' Gianni concluded.

And that little bubble of happiness simply burst right there and then. Her incredible ring cast a fiery rainbow across the table as the light caught it. Not this woman, Gianni, Jo reflected ruefully. You don't have a clue what *this* woman you're marrying wants. And that was hardly surprising when she barely knew herself.

She wouldn't be putting him on trial as a husband, no, she *wasn't*, she reasoned unhappily. She was protecting herself, refusing to give way to his apparent belief that any woman would just fall into bed with him the minute he asked. Jo, he's a gorgeous, young billionaire, she conceded grudgingly, of course he has lofty expectations that whatever he wants, he will receive. Only marriage should be different, shouldn't it? Equal partners and all that. Gianni would have to make an effort. Was it humanly possible that he had *never* had to make an effort to persuade a woman into bed before?

Gianni did not savour the chilly welcome of a cold shower instead of a warm companion in his bed that night. He was still in shock at Jo's conditions. He hadn't been prepared for Jo to dream up something that Machiavellian. No sex. And yet she wanted him. He knew that. He had felt that desire in her just the same as his own.

Why would any adult woman make sex such a stumbling block? Sex was sex...a mere bodily function, an exercise of simple pleasure, Gianni reasoned in bewilderment. Was it some religious thing with her? He was utterly mystified by her attitude. Around him, women usually couldn't wait to shed their clothes. Now he was marrying one who was making a hard limit of the one thing he was almost convinced he couldn't live without... and if that was a little glimpse of his future as a respectably married man, he was not impressed by the view.

CHAPTER FOUR

'It *is* the most gorgeous dress,' Liz Hamilton said softly with pride as she surveyed her granddaughter in her full bridal regalia.

Jo examined her reflection with a rare streak of satisfaction at her appearance. Her gown was quintessentially feminine and the instant it had appeared on the laptop screen set before her, it had stolen her heart. Pearls encrusted the lace corset bodice while the long, narrow skirt descended into fluffy ruffles that showed only a hint of her lace-covered high heels. Long lace gloves completed the look. A lightweight but superbly elegant pearl tiara anchored her upswept hair, courtesy of the pearl set Gianni had removed from his safe and offered her.

But then, Gianni had everything at his fingertips. She had been unaware, prior to their wedding plans, that Gianni utilised his personal wealth in promising investments. He co-owned an internationally famous wedding company, just as he co-owned many of the local businesses—almost everything from the nearest supermarket to the blacksmith's forge had a Renzetti stake in it. Gianni kept horses and ensuring the necessary services were available made sense. Jo had always wondered why their village seemed to be more populated and prosperous than others nearby and only now did she understand that Renzetti gold powered their presence and success.

The day after she had agreed to marry Gianni the wedding planner from London had arrived to organise everything, from her gown right down to the colour of the napkins at the reception to be held at Belvedere in the ballroom. Professional caterers had been hired. Expense was not an issue with *anything*! And that was such a total shock from Jo's point of view because she had never lived in a world in which cost was immaterial. Money had always been in short supply at Ladymead and giving up that mindset was a challenge for her. Initially, Gianni's lifestyle and spending habits had struck her pious soul as wasteful. Sybil, however, had talked her round with common sense, asking her if she was seriously expecting Gianni to live any way other than with the fabulous opulence that was all he had known since birth. And, of course, that had changed her attitude because she could not imagine Gianni without his spectacular car collection, his stable of thoroughbreds, his discreet security detail or his designer suits.

One surprise had, however, awaited her when she went to her family's lawyer to check through the prenuptial contract she was to sign before the wedding. There in bold print she had read that the renovation that her family home required, and which Gianni was financing, meant that Gianni had stipulated that their marriage had to last a minimum of five years. That had been unexpected but also just a little gratifying. She had wondered whether or not she should tackle him about that clause.

Did that clause mean that Gianni was ensuring that they stayed together for at least five years for his own personal reasons? Or was it merely the act of a shrewd businessman, who knew that fixing Ladymead's many deficiencies would cost a fortune and wanted to ensure that he received the fullest possible benefit from his convenient marriage?

Whichever reason had motivated Gianni, Jo had decided not to question it. After all, what difference did it make to her when she had decided to marry him for the sake of her family home and her relatives? And in five years' time, she told herself staunchly, even if Gianni chose to divorce her, she would still only be twenty-nine years old, an age at which she could more easily move on and make another life for herself, other than that of being a Renzetti wife.

'It's not the dress, it's *you* in the dress who is gorgeous,' Sybil insisted fondly as she escorted her great-niece out to the wedding car where her grandmother now awaited her.

'Let's hope Gianni thinks so too,' Jo quipped nervously, because it was his reaction to her appearance that mattered most to her.

And why was that? she asked herself in exasperation. Her thoughts and her emotional involvement in her wedding day were utterly inappropriate for a woman making a marriage of convenience. She wasn't about to marry some man whom she loved, she reminded herself. She liked Gianni. She found him physically attractive. But that was all, absolutely *all*, she assured herself firmly. Getting too attached to Gianni Renzetti would be sheer insanity in such a relationship, one based on practicality more than anything else.

You *are* a gold-digger, a little voice whispered deep inside her and she tensed even more. It didn't matter that Gianni didn't see her that way at present—who could tell what future changes would occur in their relationship? After all, she was marrying him for his wealth and what that wealth could do for her family and Ladymead.

'I can feel you trembling beside me,' her grandmother said worriedly, grasping Jo's cold hand. 'What on earth is the matter?'

Jo turned with a soothing smile she thought worthy of an award and replied, 'I suppose I'm just realising what a big step marriage is.'

'All that matters at the end of the day is that you love each other, and, the way Gianni looks at you, I have no doubt concerning his feelings,' the older woman responded calmly.

Neither Trixie nor her grandmother had doubted that Jo and Gianni's sudden plan to get married related to anything less than a passionate romance. Of course, both her grandmother and her great-aunt were a little naïve in that line, Jo conceded guiltily. Sybil was infinitely more worldly-wise than either.

Mercifully, Gianni had put on a good show when he had been invited over to supper one evening and that hospitality had been returned by a lavish dinner for her family at Belvedere on another night. Yes, Gianni was a smooth act when it came to such familial stuff. He had taken a video of Duffy singing his *Cabaret* phrases. He had brought another bone for McTavish. He had even let Trixie perform a tarot reading for them both, although at one stage of that rather melodramatic show from her great-aunt Jo had realised that Gianni was trying awfully hard not to laugh out loud. That had been when Trixie had forecast that he would be the father of twins within the year...

The village church loomed in front of the wedding car. It had been a very short drive as the church was built at the edge of village and the Belvedere estate, funded by the original Renzetti, who had built the house. It was a picturesque Edwardian building surrounded in well-tended lawn and seasonal summer flowers. Jo slid out of the car, careful not to soil her dainty shoes, ruffles or gloves. She rested her hand on her grandmother's arm.

'You knocked it right out of the park this time,' Gianni's best man murmured, staring down the aisle. 'She's lovely.'

Gianni turned his darkly handsome profile and saw his bride. The entire outfit somehow contrived to be the sexiest wedding gown he had ever seen. He wondered if it was the gloves, or the fact that almost every inch of her creamy skin was covered, or that the inescapably elegant line of her slender figure was revealed. He shouldn't be thinking in those terms, he reminded himself grimly, not without a wedding night ahead. Of course, she could still change her mind...

That single glimpse of Gianni as he turned, the very image of stunning dark good looks, perfectly groomed in formal attire, made Jo's mouth run even drier. Her breasts tightened, an uncomfortable ache stirring between her thighs in a way that only made her more apprehensive than ever of what their marriage would mean. She didn't want Gianni to know how much he attracted her and certainly that nobody else had ever had the same effect on her. No way was she planning to make herself into another one of the little toys he took so briefly into his bed. She was worth more than that, way more!

Sunshine cascaded through the stained-glass windows high above the altar, creating a myriad tiny rainbows to dance over the interior. The elderly priest of their parish began the service and the formal vows. Gianni had requested a short service while Jo would have preferred the longer one, but she had kept quiet on that score, reminding herself that they were a fake bridal couple in most ways and only pretending to love and care for each other. In such a ceremony, only the formalities had to be observed.

Gianni threaded the ring on her finger, his heart beating very fast. Her gossamer-fine lace gloves ended at the knuckle, anchored only by the thumb. She repeated the gesture for him. He glanced at the gleaming ring on his hand with a compressed mouth and a stormy look in his dark eyes, recalling his father's satisfaction when he had announced his plans, wondering why his parent should be so pleased that he should enter an institution that had brought the older man no personal happiness that his son had ever seen.

Jo had to almost trot to stay level with her new husband as he sped them back down the aisle, reluctantly pausing for formal photos while those waiting outside with their phones were immediately approached by security to request that the image be deleted. Gianni hurried her on into the waiting limousine.

'You look very beautiful,' Gianni murmured once they were alone. 'And for some reason I find those gloves outrageously sexy, *cara*.'

Jo went pink. 'You always know the right thing to say,' she told him, knowing that there was no way on earth she could ever tell him that her heart had stuttered inside her chest when she'd first seen him awaiting her at the altar.

She refused to give Gianni the impression that she reacted to him like some infatuated teenager…even if it was true. She reckoned most women had frivolous thoughts on their wedding days but she was very conscious that she had no excuse to behave the same way. Attraction was one thing, anything more out of the question. She wasn't planning to fall down that rabbit hole for Gianni in a marriage that she assumed would last no more than five years. She wasn't queuing up to get a broken heart, because she wasn't that stupid. That confirmed in her head, she relaxed a little.

'You don't like weddings, do you?' she remarked as they emerged from the limo outside Belvedere, a line of catering staff, headed by a smiling Abigail, already awaiting them.

'Not much. I don't think I believe in that happily ever after stuff,' he quipped. 'Too much cheating and too many divorces in my social circle.'

'You mix with the wrong people,' Jo countered. 'My grandparents were married for over fifty years.'

'They had fewer choices and temptations than the people I know,' Gianni traded, unconvinced.

And there was no time for any further personal chat because they were plunged straight into greeting guests. Some very beautiful women in fabulous dresses and jewellery were attending but equally, from the snatches of dialogue she heard around Gianni, it was almost a business occasion for an equal number of men.

Sybil strolled in with Federico Renzetti, his hand resting at her spine, and Jo resisted the urge to give her glamorous great-aunt a warning look to keep her flirtations out of the family circle. That ship had already sailed, after all. Some years earlier, Federico had invited Sybil out to dinner and she had gone, only to say that once was enough because all Gianni's father had been able to talk about was his late wife, whom he had remained obsessed with.

'And, as I remember it, Isabella treated him like dirt beneath her feet!' Sybil had commented at the time. 'Maybe that old "treat them mean, keep them keen" saying works better than you think.'

They took their seats in the ballroom at a traditional top table.

'I don't feel married yet,' Gianni murmured silkily.

'Wait until I start nagging,' Jo advised with a wide smile as she sipped her champagne, relieved that the most formal part of the day was over.

'My father's chatting up Sybil,' Gianni groaned.

'Don't worry about it. He had his chance with her and he blew it years ago.'

'Is that so?' Gianni did not hide his surprise. 'What happened?'

'Apparently, he could only talk about how much he missed your mother.'

Gianni tensed. 'I doubt that. He didn't treat her very well while she was alive.'

Aware she was treading on sensitive ground, Jo shrugged. 'I'm only repeating what Sybil told my grandmother back then. Who knows?'

'He was a terrible husband,' Gianni informed her.

Jo nodded. 'But don't forget, there's two sides to every story.'

'And what's that supposed to mean?'

Jo raised a finely arched brow, her sapphire eyes questioning his sharp tone. 'Only what I said. I know they weren't a happy couple, but you have to be fair. Your mother was ill for a good deal of their marriage and that must have imposed immense strain on them both.'

'It's none of your business.' In reality, Gianni was shaken that he himself had never grasped that obvious truth about his parents' relationship.

Jo dealt him a pained glance and turned her head away, her profile taut. He had a terrible relationship with his father, and she wasn't surprised because both men avoided discussing anything that might have improved it. She had watched Gianni greet his father almost like a stranger when he'd first arrived, and it had disturbed her. In her opinion, life was too short to cherish that kind of bias but, even so, she resolved never to mention his parents again. Unfortunately, Gianni's views were set in stone and he saw his mother as a misunderstood saint and his father as a dreadful man. He had never, she registered ruefully, really moved an inch on that issue since his mother's death when he was thirteen.

'I apologise. I was rude and you made a good point,' Gianni murmured half under his breath.

'I'm too outspoken sometimes,' Jo said lightly. 'We tend to speak the truth and shame the devil in my family.'

'While the Renzetti men barely speak at all,' Gianni completed wryly.

'That could be a point of contention between us,' Jo admitted quietly. 'I like to talk things out.'

Gianni grasped her tiny fingers and sighed. 'Why do you always foresee problems? Why aren't you more optimistic?'

'I suppose I'm just too practical. I'll work on it,' Jo promised, her plump pink lips parting in a wide smile.

Desire flashed through Gianni with the efficiency of a lightning strike. He gritted his teeth in annoyance because that level of susceptibility made him feel as though he had been plunged back into adolescence. Every time he looked at his bride, he wanted her. Of course, it was only because his libido was on a hair trigger because he hadn't had sex in so long, he reasoned with assurance. That was the *sole* reason. The scandal in the tabloid newspaper had appeared many weeks after the actual incident had taken place. In that interim period, shocked by the manner in which he had been targeted and set up for blackmail, Gianni had concentrated on the police investigation and had slept alone.

A famous singer entertained their guests during the meal. The wedding cake was cut and then Gianni swung Jo out onto the dance floor. He drew her close. The tangy aroma of his cologne mingled with his underlying scent of masculinity and warmth and she breathed in deep, with colour flaring in her cheeks. Was it pheromones or some such thing? she wondered. Because he smelt amazing to her… so amazing that she wanted to bury her nose in his jacket and just stay there.

'You're very quiet,' he complained above her head.

'Just relaxing,' Jo proffered, hoping her flush died off before they left the floor because she loathed the fact that she still blushed like a schoolgirl, having assumed that would be something she left behind after she passed her teen years.

With every movement on the floor the contact between their bodies seemed to increase, the shift of his lean hips fluid against hers, the strength and breadth of his chest pressing on her breasts. Sexual heat stole into her like a thief in the night, lighting up a glow in all her sensitive areas. She made excuses for herself. Aside from that single kiss, they had never been so close before. But he was aroused as well. That awareness made her feel less awkward and even made her hide a smile against his shoulder. It was strange, she reflected, how something that had made her uncomfortable with other men somehow enthralled her when it was Gianni in the starring role.

And possibly more than a little naïve, she admonished herself for, aside from his veneration of his mother's memory, Gianni seemed to have little interest in women beyond sexual satisfaction. She had sort of guessed that about him when he had changed girlfriends at head-turning speed as a teenager and teenaged beauties with broken hearts had littered the neighbourhood. Back then gossip had always kept her up to date with Gianni's extracurricular activities, but that handy conduit of information had died once he went to university. Once again, she found herself wondering who that first and only love of his had been. As far as the gossip columns were concerned, he had dated no woman for long, so the likelihood was that he had fallen in love as a student.

Questioning her own intense curiosity, Jo suppressed it. What did the whys and wherefores of Gianni's one and only love matter to her? It was none of her business, and cultivating an interest in such things would only lead to friction in their relationship, but he was too reserved a guy to share confidences.

Later that afternoon, she went upstairs to change because they were leaving soon to fly out to Italy. Sybil was smiling and unusually cheerful.

'Federico flirting up a storm?' Jo teased. 'It's always nice to be appreciated.'

'I've got goss about his marriage,' Sybil revealed. 'I think he only told me because he wants me to eat out with him again but this lady's not for turning.'

'I'm not sure I should listen to it,' Jo confided ruefully. 'Gianni is still so sensitive about his unhappy childhood, not that he would even admit that it *was* unhappy.'

'He's got to have the odd flaw or two. His parents' marriage was a disaster,' Sybil opined. 'The year before Federico met Isabella, the love of Isabella's life, the man she *planned* to marry, died in a plane crash. Her father threatened to leave his fortune to another relative if she didn't find a husband and that's why she married Federico. He didn't find that out until years afterwards. She closed the bedroom door after Gianni was conceived and it never opened again. She just used him!'

Jo wriggled out of her wedding gown and laid it carefully on the bed. 'I hate taking it off.'

'Gianni should be playing maid here, not me!' Sybil quipped. 'No comment about what I just told you? I think that if Gianni knew those facts, he wouldn't be so hard on his father.'

'His father should tell his son himself,' Jo said prosaically. 'I'm not going to get involved. Are you planning to see Federico again?'

'I haven't decided yet. He hasn't stayed at Belvedere since Gianni took official ownership a few years back. It's wicked that Isabella even took this house from Federico. She put so much money into fixing it up after their marriage that she demanded he sign it over to her.'

It was news to Jo that the Renzettis had ever been that short of cash and she simply sighed, thinking that Federico had known how to forge a path into Sybil's heavily guarded heart. Just as she rescued stray animals, Sybil liked to rescue people. 'You feel sorry for him,' she said softly.

'How could I not? Isabella fooled us all into thinking she was so vulnerable and poorly treated, but her husband also suffered. His wife didn't love him, she only loved her son and Federico's only child doesn't even *like* him!' Sybil proclaimed with spirit.

'Perhaps he should put more effort into talking to his son.' And that was Jo's last word on the subject, for it seemed that her great-aunt saw a softer side to Federico Renzetti than others did for, even as a child, Jo had found the older man cold and silent. Evidently, Sybil had the power to turn him into a positive chatterbox. She herself barely knew the man and had no opinion to offer.

Sheathed in a midnight-blue sundress, her feet in high-heeled sandals, Jo accompanied her aunt down the huge wide staircase that ornamented Belvedere's marble front hall where a few clusters of guests, who had left the ballroom, stood around talking and drinking. Lounging in a chair at the back of the hall with his father, Gianni sprang immediately upright, a smile lightening his taut, dark expression, and strode forward.

At the foot of the stairs, a woman intercepted Jo.

'What have you got that I haven't got?' the woman demanded imperiously and very loudly, her champagne glass wavering in her hand. 'That's what I want to know!'

'Sorry, I—' Jo moved to sidestep the clearly inebriated woman.

'It's a simple question, answer it,' the woman slurred, heads swivelling all around them. 'I got one night with Gianni and then I sat wasting my time and waiting for a phone call that never came.'

'This isn't the time or the place for this, my dear,' Sybil interposed. 'Let's return to the ballroom.'

'No, I want the bride to answer me!' the blonde ranted even louder, her expression one of desperation, her face tear-stained as she closed her hand over Jo's wrist to prevent her from walking away from her. 'Hell, you're beautiful, anyone can see that, but what special quality do you have?'

'Milly, how lovely to see you again,' Gianni interrupted smooth as glass as he signalled someone. 'Jojo's special quality is that I love her. '

Milly looked at him as though he had stuck a knife in her heart, her eyes overflowing, tears trailing down her quivering cheeks just as one of Gianni's security men approached, clearly intending to remove her from the house.

'No, it's all right, Milly,' Jo said gently as the hand fell from her wrist and the other woman's head lowered in defeat and embarrassment. 'Let's go somewhere quiet where you can sit down and relax while we find your friends.'

As the security man hovered and Gianni froze, bewildered by his bride's unexpected intervention, Jo walked the weeping woman across the hall into the nearest room, knowing that Sybil would ensure that Milly's companions were located to take care of her.

'You'll have to try to be kinder,' Sybil warned Gianni on her way past him again. 'Jo has a huge heart.'

Gianni had said he loved her with such panache even though they both knew it was a lie, Jo reflected as she left the distraught woman with her friend, who had made many apologies for her, dismissed as unnecessary by Jo. People got drunk, upset, sometimes forgot themselves and said stuff they shouldn't. That was life even at a luxury bridal occasion at Belvedere. But the other woman's pain had wounded Jo. She couldn't help wondering how many other women her bridegroom had hurt over the years and supposed that there would be quite a few with disappointed hopes. Well, she wasn't going to be one of them, she promised herself. No way was she going to fall for him!

Impervious to Sybil's advice, Gianni only waited until the limousine door had closed on them to say, 'What on earth possessed you to take that woman aside after she had insulted you?'

'She didn't insult me. She was drunk, hurt, bitter, jealous. *Your* doing,' Jo murmured with succinct bite. 'That's the other side of the coin to your lifestyle.'

Gianni slung her an incredulous appraisal. 'We're *not* discussing this.'

'Of course not.' Jo had expected exactly that response, but she hoped she had made him think about the damage that could result from his enjoyment of his freedom and a wide variety of women.

'You should have stood back and allowed my security men to handle her in a more appropriate manner,' Gianni imparted curtly.

Jo said nothing. She inclined her head, dug a fat book out of her new capacious leather bag in her favourite shade of electric blue and read all the way to the airport.

Gianni breathed in deep and slow, mastering his temper. *His* lifestyle? His former lifestyle had been destroyed the minute he put that wedding ring on her finger and he did not appreciate having his past sins thrown in his teeth the same day. In any case, it was not as though he planned to emulate his father and keep a mistress, an act that had broken his mother's heart. Even if he didn't love Jojo, he would be a good husband. At least she hadn't preached at him about his sexually adventurous past. Evidently her sympathies were with the woman. But he hadn't wronged anyone! He hadn't seduced Milly or done anything questionable with her either! For a long few minutes, Gianni quietly simmered.

Eventually, he registered that for once in his life, he had been naïve to believe that he could marry Jo Hamilton without experiencing moments of frustration. In comparison to him she had led a very clean, God-fearing life. They had lived at opposite ends of the worldly spectrum and naturally cherished very different views. Yet, he still respected Jojo more than any woman he had ever met. He liked her brand of refreshing honesty, her quick intelligence *and* her strong streak of compassion. Another bride might have thrown a scene about her perfect day being ruined by a former lover of the groom, might, indeed, have taken her resentment out on him. Jojo had done neither. No, she had empathised with the other woman. Unbelievable, he thought wryly, and yet it had happened…

Jo had never travelled in a private jet before, indeed had only enjoyed a handful of trips abroad, all relating to school organised trips. Now she was seated in an opulent cabin furnished like a very superior office with comfortable cream leather seating, even recliners. Magazines had been brought to her and a menu of refreshments tendered by an efficient steward. Like so many of the rich trappings of Gianni's life, it felt like another world to Jo.

'We're heading for my mother's family home on Isola di Cristoforo,' Gianni explained as they left the jet in Italy only to board a helicopter. 'It's an old property and the island enjoys a rich history with several ancient ruins. I thought you would enjoy it.'

'Is that a crack about the money pit that is now your responsibility?' Jo joked, because temporary repairs to secure Ladymead were already taking place. Her relatives were now discussing whether or not they would move out during the extensive renovations because Gianni had offered them a village house for the duration of the work to be done.

'Not at all. I merely thought it would give you an interest for a honeymoon that's not really a honeymoon,' Gianni remarked.

Jo reddened and wished she had kept quiet, because of course theirs wouldn't be the traditional honeymoon that most couples enjoyed.

She craned her neck but only saw a dizzying view of mature trees as the helicopter descended. When she emerged, she glimpsed stone walls through the tree trunks.

'It's a medieval castle,' Gianni told her with amusement. 'My mother's father owned the island and my mother told me that he revelled in his fortress on the hill as a symbol of his power. I'm a rare visitor and most of the island is a nature reserve now and open to the public. I never knew him. All my grandparents were gone by the time I was four years old. I envy your close ties with your grandmother.'

'That's because Gran's really been my mother,' Jo explained as they arrived at giant double doors standing open in the sunshine in readiness for their arrival. 'But I'm probably closest to Sybil. My great-aunts were still quite young when Gran got married and the sisters have always lived together.'

'My father thought it was a rum set-up in your household—three sisters and one man.'

Jo shrugged. 'It worked for all of them. The house was large enough. Grandpa was a bit like a father to Sybil and Trixie, although Trixie was already a teenager. Families stayed together in those days. Grandpa married Gran knowing her sisters came with her.'

'People still mention him. Your grandfather was well liked.'

An older woman with greying hair greeted them in Italian in the medieval hall with its stone walls hung with imposing family portraits. Gianni took charge of showing Jo upstairs, opening an oak door on an elegant room furnished with a scarlet-draped four-poster bed. Flowers were scattered across the quilt and beautiful ivory blooms were massed in several vases throughout the large room.

Jo's sapphire blue eyes widened. 'My goodness. It's lovely.'

'It's been set up for our wedding night. I'm sleeping next door,' Gianni informed her as her luggage was brought in. 'I understand that dinner will be served in an hour on the terrace.'

Jo went pink. Gianni stalked towards her, spectacularly lithe, lean and darkly handsome, his stunning dark golden eyes welded to her hot face. 'But when our marriage becomes normal, I will demand that you put on that beautiful dress and those gloves again just for me one evening,' he imparted silkily.

Her blue eyes flew wide, and her generous lips curved. 'It's a deal,' she almost whispered, relieved by his attitude.

'We've got everything going for us, *cara*. You married me in the wake of that scandal and I appreciate that,' he admitted in a driven undertone as if such an admission did not come easily to him.

'And I appreciate you being…understanding,' Jo selected awkwardly.

'Kissing still on the menu?' Gianni surveyed her with dark eyes glittering below a lush canopy of black lashes and her heart skipped a beat.

'Of course,' she muttered tightly, barely able to get air into her lungs.

His arms closed round her and her heart began to pound as if she were running a race. He tipped her face up, covered her mouth with his and teased her sensitive lips with the tip of his tongue, igniting a fierce desire in her for more. But she couldn't have more…she knew that. Gianni needed a challenge with a reward. He knew that himself. He was already practically training McTavish into begging at his feet out of sheer greed. And not in this lifetime did she plan to find herself begging at Gianni's feet as so many others of her sex had done before. His fingers strummed down her spine and a wanton shiver ran through her entire body, her breasts peaking, her thighs pressing together. Out of the question, she reminded herself angrily.

She pulled back from him and smiled soothingly. 'Sorry, but I'm desperate for a shower before dinner.'

Gianni's gorgeous eyes flashed like the shimmer of pure gold in sunlight, much as if she had thrown him a challenge. 'I'll see you downstairs, then, *cara.*'

He was so smooth, so practised, it was impossible to shift him out of automatic charming mode, she mused ruefully as she freshened up. But she needed much more from him than that polished surface show.

The next morning, Jo stirred drowsily, voices filtering out from somewhere bringing her eyes open.

As she woke up, she recalled the beautiful meal she had shared with Gianni the night before and the guilty enchantment of the wedding day that was already behind her. Her spirits were buoyant after a long and very necessary deep sleep in an incredibly comfortable bed. She went into the bathroom and washed before tugging on a light robe to head downstairs. She didn't have to get fully dressed first thing, did she? Gianni was always so laid-back. She didn't need to dot every i and cross every t for his benefit.

It was only when she reached the stone stairs that she realised that there were two male voices speaking very loudly in Italian towards the rear of the castle. Indeed, they weren't speaking, they were shouting in what sounded like a bitter argument. What on earth was happening? she wondered as she followed the voices to source.

Jo was astonished to cross the threshold of the room Gianni used as an office and find herself in the midst of a heated dispute between Gianni and his father.

As the two men focused on her, both fell ominously silent.

'What on earth's going on?' she exclaimed.

Federico Renzetti turned his censorious gaze on her with disdain. 'Perhaps that's something *you* could clarify for our benefit.'

CHAPTER FIVE

'*ME?*' JO ECHOED in disbelief, wondering what on earth *she* could possibly have to do with their argument.

Gianni looked at Jo as he had never looked at her in his life before: with furious distaste and condemnation.

'This is my fault, *all* my fault,' Federico muttered in a pained declaration as he shot a guilty glance in his son's direction. 'I persuaded you to get married and, like you, I too would have believed that you had made a very safe and sensible choice of wife.'

Jo was not slow on the uptake and that statement was an attack on her integrity. 'I don't know what you are talking about,' she told her father-in-law. 'But I think it's time that I did.'

Gianni strode across to his desk and punched a hand down on the crumpled newspaper lying there. His dark golden gaze was lit up like the hot, stormy heart of a bonfire.

Jo raised a brow. 'Words, Gianni...*words*,' she urged.

In a violent movement he swept up the newspaper and thrust it at her, drama accompanying his very gesture. 'Read it and weep!' he advised. 'You've been exposed as the fake you truly are!'

Although shaken by his attitude, Jo remained outwardly composed. She grasped the newspaper and registered that it was the same sleazy publication that had published the article on Gianni's worst mistake. It was a misunderstanding, Jo told herself, a ghastly, embarrassing misunderstanding. What else could it be? She didn't have any enemies that she knew about and had nothing in her past that she wished to conceal. Her knees loosened when she recognised the photo of Ralph's one-time fiancée, Jane Yerry. Not a pleasant girl. Jo had gone to school with the attractive brunette, who had been a terrible bully. But what on earth could Jane have to say about her? Her phone was vibrating madly in the pocket of her robe and it was a challenge to ignore it while two angry men stared at her as if they were expecting her to spontaneously combust or breakdown.

Instead, Jo backed down into an armchair on wobbly knees to address her attention to the newspaper. As she read, she was instantly infuriated by Jane's vile claim that Ralph had cheated on her with Jo and that Jo was the reason why Jane's engagement had been broken off. In one corner there was also a photo of Gianni and Jo emerging from the village church after their wedding, the only part of the day when camera phones had been less restricted.

'This is a load of bilge,' she spelt out unhappily, because she was affronted to find herself the target of such lies in print even though she was conscious that just about all the people who knew her and the other parties concerned were also aware of the *true* story.

My goodness, she reflected wretchedly, why the heck would Jane make up such outrageous lies? Her brow furrowing, she contemplated that puzzle. Jane had never been a fan of Jo's longstanding friendship with Ralph and Jo had been careful to stay in the background once she had recognised that reality.

Sadly, that broken engagement had, in the

end, turned out very badly for Jane Yerry. Ralph had turned his back after discovering her in bed with his best friend, Peter, but Peter had been shamed into walking away from Jane as well. Jane's parents had been outraged by their daughter's conduct and by the cost of cancelling a large wedding at the very last minute. Jo's ongoing friendship with Ralph afterwards and the rumours that they were actually together as a couple would have annoyed Jane. Evidently hearing talk about Jo's marriage to one of the richest men in the country had ignited Jane's bitterness and she had made a crazy attempt to rescue her own reputation at the cost of Jo's. Even so, while Jo would not have counted Jane a friend, she would not have believed her to be an enemy either.

'I'm at a loss to understand why Jane would make such claims to a newspaper,' Jo confided quietly. 'But I think she'll find she's made a major mistake because most people will be annoyed with her for trying to shift the blame for her broken engagement onto me.'

Both men studied her with varying degrees of disbelief.

'And that's all you have to say on this subject?' Federico Renzetti pressed almost delicately.

'I do not even know who these people are!' Gianni told Jo.

'Why would you?' Jo responded, her tone even softer. 'And why would you even care about this nonsense?'

'Nonsense?' Gianni fired at her wrathfully. 'My bride's reputation has been trashed!'

His father measured the flash of Jo's steady sapphire gaze and said, 'You must understand. Gianni *married* you to rehabilitate his image. Being plunged back into another scandal is not what he expected or even prepared for.'

'Possibly *you* don't understand that I don't intend to shoulder any responsibility for someone telling bold and wicked lies about me,' Jo cut in curtly, her apparent composure lurching because she had not been ready for the older man to instantly throw the reason for their marriage in her face. It struck her that her father-in-law had judged her guilty the instant he'd learned of the tabloid piece even if he was being less obvious about the fact than Gianni was. But no, it wasn't possible that Gianni could believe such a character assassination, she reasoned. Gianni *knew* her. He knew her nature, her moral outlook. He could not possibly credit that she could have slept with Ralph behind Jane's back… *could he*?

'Obviously, you're going to say that it's all lies…and yet you did step into that woman's shoes after he ended things with her,' Gianni reminded her very drily. 'Even if I didn't know you or much about anyone involved, you wouldn't be the first woman to lie to me.'

Losing colour, Jo jerked shakily upright. 'I'm not having this conversation with you in your father's presence. I'm going upstairs to get dressed.'

'I'm returning to London immediately,' the older man declared with a hint of awkwardness and regret that ironically made her like him a tiny bit better. Most particularly, when her bridegroom was still regarding her much as if she had suddenly sprouted hooves and horns. What was the matter with Gianni? What had happened to his quick and clever brain?

As Gianni alerted the pilot to return his father to the airport, he was reeling in shock. Federico had arrived at the castle barely thirty minutes earlier and yet Gianni, famous for his fast reactions, was *still* reeling in shock and disgust. He could not explain to his own satisfaction why he felt so shattered by what that newspaper story had told him. Jo's coolness under fire had merely made him more suspicious, giving him an unwelcome view of his bride as a practised dissembler. Why had he been so convinced that Jo was the exact opposite of most of the other women he had known?

Why the hell, when he had previously been such a cynic, *had* he decided that Josephine Hamilton was in an entirely different category from the liars, swindlers and gold-diggers who littered his own past?

After all, liars and adulterers came in all shapes and sizes. Gianni had seen enough men and women behaving badly over the years to know that. Unluckily for her, Gianni had a particular aversion to the disloyal, dishonest, and unfaithful, having seen his own father in that guise from childhood. And he could not deny that the idea of Jo sneaking around behind backs to sleep with a man engaged to another woman filled him with rampant revulsion.

But why was he *so* angry?

It was her past, it was before they had even got together *and* the guy was dead and buried, the saner side of his mind argued. But it didn't change his mood one iota. He was furious with Jo for ripping apart his good-living image of her and he was furious with himself for being savagely disappointed in her. He had genuinely believed that she was above such behaviour and incredibly honest, only nasty reality had washed a film of grime over that conviction.

Even so, in his heart, Gianni did know *why* he was so enraged. He had believed in Jo, admired her character, even begun to like her. And although it was most unlike him, he had somehow managed to place Jo on a very tall pedestal. Regrettably, she had fallen off it with a resounding crash and it had happened so fast that his mind was still spinning with a sense of incredulity. Initially, he had had a ferocious argument with Federico and had been ready to defend Jo until his dying breath…and then he had read that article and tied it in with what he already knew. And the awareness that he could still be so gullible as to place that amount of faith in a woman's honour and decency hugely embarrassed him.

Worst of all, however, he told himself bitterly, the reason he had married her had become redundant for there was no way her grubby affair with a man promised to another woman could clean up his image. That meant that he had also taken on the money pit on false pretences. Federico had warned him that he was insane to take on Ladymead without setting a strict budget, but then his father had never enjoyed the kind of wealth that his son had inherited. And something about Jo had made Gianni, usually the shrewd businessman when it came to cost, want to be as generous as proved necessary. He tossed back a second brandy without savouring the vintage.

Upstairs in her bedroom, Jo was all fingers and thumbs as she fought her way into linen shorts and a tee. Gianni was acting crazy, she reflected in consternation. He hadn't asked her any questions; he had simply assumed that that horrible story was the truth. Did she strike him as that kind of woman? Or was that distrust innate in him with women?

She was shaken by the way he had looked at her and acted. She hadn't recognised him in that angry mood, all warmth and familiarity stripped from him, and all that did was make her wonder if she had *ever* had a clue as to what really went on inside Gianni.

But how dared he behave like that?

A little voice at the back of her brain reminded her that she had chosen not to tell him that her true relationship with Ralph had been platonic. On some foolish level, had she preferred to let Gianni believe that she had had, at least, *one* serious relationship? Jo paled at that glimpse inside herself where she suddenly recognised her insecurity. She was insecure with Gianni because he was infinitely more experienced and sophisticated than she would ever be.

Nobody knew better than Jo that she had led a sheltered life, surrounded by outdated rules and protected by her family. Circumstances had confined her at Ladymead, depriving her of the independent choices and freedom that many young adults took for granted. Even as a student she had lived at home because it was so much cheaper to do so. And although she would not have brandished the fact, she suspected that she was naturally rather unadventurous in her habits. Marrying Gianni was far and away the most dangerous step and the biggest risk she had ever taken.

In point of fact, she acknowledged with piercing dismay, she and Gianni were a bad match with almost nothing in common. What did that leave her to work with when they had a dispute? He was burning up like a Roman torch and she was striving to stay calm and collected even though her tummy was lurching with nausea.

Jo went back into Gianni's study. He was standing at the doors open onto the terrace with his back turned to her. 'We need to sort this misunderstanding out,' she told him bravely.

Gianni swung round to face her, his lean, strong face grim. 'I'm not stupid, *cara*. This is no misunderstanding.'

Frustration currented through Jo, putting her even more on edge. 'I didn't have an affair with Ralph and if you'd ever met Ralph, you would know that. Jane's lying. She's the one who had the affair that made Ralph break off their engagement.'

'Isn't it strange how you never mentioned any of this before?' Gianni sliced in, his wide mouth flattening, his narrowed dark eyes hard and unyielding. 'You never acknowledged that Ralph even *had* a previous engagement, and it wasn't referred to at the funeral either—'

'Why would it have been mentioned?' It was Jo's turn to interrupt, an edge of panic gaining inside her because she knew he wasn't listening to her. 'Ralph dumping Jane and *her* infidelity kept the gossipmongers busy for months and he was horribly embarrassed and hurt by the whole business. Nobody was likely to mention that broken engagement.'

'I don't want to hear about Ralph or your grubby affair with him and I'm not interested either in hearing your counter-accusations against this Yerry woman,' Gianni incised chillingly. 'In one sense what you chose to get up to prior to our marriage is nothing to do with me, but in another it's very much *my* business. I married you to clean up my image. I believed that you had a spotless reputation. That's the only reason I married you.'

Pale as milk at that cutting clarification, Jo lifted her head high and tilted her chin. 'I'm sorry if you don't feel that you got value for money,' she murmured flatly.

'That's not what I said, but it does express something of what I feel now,' Gianni confessed in a raw undertone, volatile dark golden eyes full of condemnation. 'I certainly wasn't expecting a twenty-two-carat virgin, but I *was* expecting a wife without a mess like this behind her and the subsequent mortification of her being exposed to derision in the media.'

Even though she hadn't done anything wrong, Jo felt shamed, as though she were responsible for Jane's deceitful attempt to rewrite history at Jo's expense. Her cheeks flamed and she swallowed hard. He was talking down to her—how dared he? But on another level, she knew that she was still traumatised from becoming the target of such a character assassination. Her phone had kept on buzzing while she was getting dressed. She had a dozen missed calls from various people and she had texted Sybil, promising to call her back later. Ralph's parents had also attempted to contact her and she would have to speak to them as well. They were quite an age and anything that disparaged their late son's character would have deeply distressed them.

'This is a storm in a teacup,' Jo declared, trying another tack with Gianni in an attempt to dial down the tension.

'It means a hell of a lot more than that to me!' Gianni fired back at her, his seething dissatisfaction blazing in dark golden eyes, semi-concealed by dense black lashes. 'I had complete faith in you and you've blown it.'

'I've done nothing, Gianni,' Jo countered steadily, holding her ground. 'Jane Yerry is lying. I didn't have an affair behind her back with her fiancé. I was *never* intimate with Ralph.'

'And how likely am I to credit that in this day and age?' Gianni derided.

'Ralph and I were only friends…at least on my side,' Jo adjusted, sticking scrupulously to the absolute truth for fear of causing further misapprehensions. 'We weren't engaged. Our supposed engagement was only a rumour, which I think he encouraged.'

'No more!' Gianni slashed a lean, powerful hand through the air, contriving somehow to express anger, disbelief and boredom all in that single gesture. 'I refuse to listen to another word of this nonsense!'

'You don't believe me,' Jo registered in consternation, blaming herself for not sooner correcting his impression that she had once been engaged to Ralph.

Gianni dipped his chin. 'I don't,' he confirmed without remorse.

'Where does that leave us, then?' she asked numbly.

Gianni lifted and dropped a broad shoulder in dismissal before striding out of the room without another word. When she heard his bedroom door close upstairs, she shivered, wondering how she was supposed to disprove Jane's contentions when she was so far away from home. A chorus of family disagreement would soon have disabused Gianni of his suspicions, but she was shaken by his inability to simply accept that she was telling the truth.

A little while later, she heard Gianni's steps on the stone stairs and hunger drove her from her room. The table below the thick canopy of vines at the front of the castle was set for lunch and she sat back in her sunglasses scanning the magnificent view of the mountainous island. Directly ahead stretched a shaded drive through an avenue of stately palm trees that led down to an empty golden strand washed by the tide. Just as she finally noticed that there was only one place set at the table, she heard the whine of the helicopter and turned to watch it fly out across the sea until it became a vanishing speck. She breathed in slow and deep and planned an exploration of the nature reserve.

Later, as she wandered along deserted winding trails, she tried not to think that her marriage had crashed and burned on the very first day. Negative thoughts were not her friend. Gianni had an explosive temperament. He needed time to think and calm down. She had known that when she married him. She had suspected that the burning passion that powered everything he did from his work ethic to his libido could also be a problem. So, she would have to fix him…somehow. Teach him to talk? Put him in a cell so that he couldn't walk away? Lock every outside door?

For the first twelve hours of his desertion, Jo was sanguine. She wandered round the island, explored the Roman ruins and she swam and lazed on the beach in the sun. The second day she was on edge, even after a long swim in the sea. And by lunchtime she was burning with a strong and rare anger.

She phoned Gianni.

He answered her call in the middle of another call and her lips compressed at the suspicion that her bridegroom had walked out on his new marriage and basically buried himself in the convenience of work. She wondered how often Gianni had buried life's problems in the world of business and straightened her slight shoulders to brace herself.

'Jojo…' he breathed tautly.

Jo didn't give him the chance to regroup. 'I'm only calling to ask you to arrange transport for me to go home—'

'Home?' he cut in, audibly taken aback by that decision. 'To Ladymead?'

'Where else? Sitting alone in luxury on a deserted island is not my idea of fun. You've gone.'

'I'm coming back.'

'When?' Jo enquired briskly. 'I have no intention of sitting here like faithful Penelope waiting on Odysseus.'

Torn between admiration that she had read Homer's *Odyssey* and shocked surprise that she was calling his bluff, Gianni murmured quietly, his accent more noticeable than usual, 'This evening…this has got out of hand.'

'And before you return,' Jo replied, 'you accept certain facts, which anyone in my family could confirm for you. I didn't have an affair with Ralph two years ago. I liked him as a friend and I felt considerable sympathy for him when he found his fiancée and his best friend in the same bed. I suspect Ralph would have liked a closer connection with me after that discovery, but I wasn't interested. His parents were aware that we were only friends and they have been hurt and offended by that newspaper article because, of course, they know the truth. They're having a lawyer's letter sent to Jane and a retraction is to be printed in the newspaper.'

There was a short, dragging silence.

'I'm sorry.'

'You have to say it in person or I don't listen,' Jo told him gently.

CHAPTER SIX

EARLY EVENING, AND THE sun was sinking in a peach-coloured sky, but summer sunshine still bathed the colourful terraced gardens in a shimmering veil of heat.

As the whine of a helicopter approaching the island sounded, Jo left her seat on the shaded roof terrace and darted over to the telescope that Gianni's late grandfather had installed to survey the island from his hilltop eyrie. Breathless, she watched the helicopter land on the pad. Seconds later, a tall male sprang out to stride along the path through the trees and her heart started to beat very, very fast.

It was Gianni, sleek and spectacular in a cream lightweight suit teamed with an open-neck dark shirt. Light glimmered over his tousled black hair, accentuating the slant of his high cheekbones, the proud jut of his nose, the mobile slash of his passionate mouth and the hard, clean, angular line of his jaw. Her breath rattled in her dry throat and then she questioned what she was doing…*spying* on him? *Waiting* for him? Disturbed by that suspicion and annoyed with herself, Jo grabbed up her book and descended the winding stone staircase to the foot of the tower before strolling, flushed and a little out of breath, out onto the loggia, surprised to see that Sofia, the housekeeper, already had the table set for two.

Gianni came to an abrupt halt on the path and flipped off his sunglasses, dark golden eyes flashing over her before his lashes lowered to conceal his expression. For the first time ever in her experience of Gianni, he looked a little hesitant.

'I was wrong. I screwed up,' he bit out in a taut undertone as though he could not bear to wait any longer to offload those necessary words. 'I'm deeply sorry.'

'I need you to explain *why* though,' Jo muttered uneasily. 'Why you were so quick to assume?'

Gianni raked long brown fingers through his hair in a gesture of frustration. 'I'm not good with words, Jojo…not when it comes to emotional stuff.'

Jo almost winced. 'I know but—'

'I suspected that buying you something would be the wrong thing to do, so I passed on the flowers,' he murmured flatly, sliding a hand into his pocket as he sidestepped her question. 'But then, as you will see, I succumbed all the same.'

Gritting her teeth in confusion at that declaration and discomfort because she didn't want Gianni thinking that he could buy his way out of trouble, Jo flipped open the jewellery box with its famous logo to reveal a delicate platinum necklace. She lifted it out to examine the diamond and sapphire studded pendant, which was in the shape of a bouquet of flowers. Gianni intervened to click open the bouquet to let her see the words engraved within.

'I'm sorry,' it said, with the addition of his name and the date.

'In case I didn't get the right words out fast enough,' he breathed tautly.

The backs of her eyes prickled horribly with a surge of tears and she blinked rapidly. 'It's very pretty. I appreciate the thought behind it,' she told him quietly. 'But, you know, you didn't need to buy me anything.'

His hand closed over hers. 'I hurt you. I do very much regret that.'

Sofia bustled out with a tray of drinks and Jo tugged her hand free. Her stiff knees began to give way to the strain of standing so unnaturally still and straight and she sank down into a padded chair, grateful to have a glass to curl her restive fingers around.

'Let me put this on for you…' Gianni lifted the necklace from the box and stepped behind her to loop the pendant round her neck and fasten it. She felt his fingertips brush her nape and a shiver of awareness shimmied down her tense spine.

'Thank you,' she said unevenly as Sofia lit the candles on the table, determined, it seemed, to make the most of what she deemed to be a romantic occasion for the *odd* couple, Jo reflected in chagrin. After all, the bride and groom had occupied separate beds on their wedding night, enjoyed a huge row the next day and that had been followed by the departure of the bridegroom.

As the older woman moved back into the building, Jo lifted her head, her blue eyes very serious. 'Why did you just assume that I was guilty?'

Gianni tensed. 'I had a blazing row with Federico when he arrived and first voiced his allegations. In the beginning, I didn't want to credit what he was telling me. I was furious with him for attacking your reputation... and then he gave me the newspaper. Unfortunately, the few facts I knew seemed to fit. I was appalled,' he admitted tautly.

Her smooth brow furrowed. 'But I don't understand why. Although I didn't do what I was accused of doing, you're not *that* narrow-minded and you yourself—'

Gianni lifted soothing hands to silence her. 'I know, but I've always seen you as being special, as being a cut above me in your behaviour. Why do you think I never tried too hard to persuade you to join me for dinner?' he asked her with gleaming dark eyes. 'I suspected that I would upset you and I was determined not to do it.'

As Sofia set a variety of tiny savoury tarts before them as a starter, Jo stared at Gianni, his words still echoing inside her head. *Special? A cut above?*

'Look,' Gianni murmured very softly. 'I

am not a gentleman and many of the women I have been with have only been ladies in the strictest sense of the word. They had few boundaries and no illusions. Their only desire was to have a good time. I know my limitations, *cara*. I knew that you and I would want different things.'

'Only until you decided that I was exactly what you needed to rehabilitate your image,' Jo reminded him as she lifted a tiny tart with determination. 'Therefore, I'm a plaster saint and you're a sinner, so you pretty much kept your distance. Actually, I'm a little more human than that, and rather more flexible and flawed.'

Luxuriant lashes dipped low over his golden gaze. 'Not as flawed as I am,' he admitted on the back of a rueful sigh. 'My whole outlook on life is pessimistic. That's why I jumped so fast to my conclusion that I had been mistaken in your character.'

Jo countered, 'You lost your head. You erupted like a volcano.'

'That my father was present put my temper on a hair trigger. It was bad enough that I should be forced to view you in such a light, even worse that he should have instigated that exposure.'

'You felt humiliated by his witnessing that scene,' Jo whispered. 'But he was upset on your behalf. I think he was trying to protect you in some clumsy way just by being there.'

'My father has never tried to protect me from anything. Eat up,' Gianni urged, sneaking another tiny tart onto her plate. 'Sofia said you've been skipping meals and you're too slender to do that.'

'I don't get very hungry when it's this warm. You contacted Sofia before your arrival,' Jo guessed then.

'I knew you wouldn't mention that I was returning.' Gianni dealt her a shrewd look. 'You didn't quite trust that I *would* return.'

Jo shrugged a slim shoulder. 'Do you blame me?'

But Jo was still struggling to come to terms with what he had already told her, shaken by what he had admitted about his view of her prior to his proposal. A woman he had seen as prim and proper and above suspicion, squeaky clean in mind and body. What did it say about her that it cut her to the bone to recognise that he had never seen her as a normal sexy, adult woman? Was it any wonder that he had really only been teasing her when he'd invited her out to dinner? She wasn't his type, had *never* been his type of woman.

'You walked out on me,' she extended tightly. 'I find that hard to forgive.'

As Sofia's daughter delivered the main course, Gianni gritted his teeth. 'I was afraid of what I might say if I stayed any longer. I felt…out of control. I thought it was wiser to leave until I had got a grip on my temper again.'

'But leaving me here…*alone*,' Jo persisted. 'That was unacceptable. I was ready to go home but I didn't know how to get off this blasted island!'

'It didn't occur to me that I was leaving you stranded.' Gianni grimaced. 'I have to learn to start thinking for two, rather than one.'

'You only need to start thinking for two if this marriage survives the first week,' Jo murmured wryly. 'And so far, we're not ripping up any record books here. When you tell me that you see me as some prim and proper prude with whom you have nothing in common—'

'Aside from a very strong attraction,' Gianni cut in. 'I'm trying to be honest, *cara*, but you finding fault with that honesty isn't any encouragement to continue in that vein.'

Jo paled. 'I didn't mean—'

'Yes, you did. You're still angry with me, which is perfectly understandable. Do you remember the first time I asked you out?'

'Vaguely,' Jo lied in a face-saving excuse because, even though six years had passed, she still vividly remembered that day. 'It seemed very random. One day I saw you at that music festival and the next—'

Gianni groaned and pushed his plate away. He leant back in his seat. 'It wasn't even slightly random. I saw you dancing at the festival with your friends.'

Jo lowered her lashes and continued to savour her tender steak. It had been *totally* random because Gianni had had a gorgeous girlfriend with him, a famous fashion model with titian curls and incredibly long porcelain limbs, who had complained throughout his attempted introduction that she was burning in the sun.

Gianni, in comparison, was recalling Jo at eighteen, sheathed in worn denim shorts and a floaty blouse, her blonde fall of sun-streaked hair bouncing at her slender spine as she danced. At the time, she had been the sexiest sight he had ever seen, the very picture of glowing health with her curvy hips shifting to the beat of the music and every inch of her unenhanced and natural. He hadn't been able to take his eyes off her and the following morning he had shown up at Ladymead, drawn by a powerful need to see her again.

Sheer lust, he labelled in retrospect. Her grandmother had directed him out to the barn where Jo had been helping Sybil to feed her rescue animals. As he'd spoken, she had stared at him as if he had taken leave of his wits and then those beautiful sapphire-blue eyes had glimmered with warmth and plea-sure. He had been so sure that she was about to say yes and his conscience had twanged accordingly, because although she had fin-ished school, he had been very much aware of her youth and inexperience in comparison to his own. And then she had said no, sorry, and a crazy mix of anger and relief had swept through him.

'I've never wanted a woman as much as I

wanted you that day,' he confessed grudgingly. 'But you weren't ready for someone like me.'

'No,' she agreed reluctantly. 'Panic made me turn you down. I didn't think I could handle you either.'

As she connected with glittering dark golden eyes fringed with a lush canopy of black lashes, her heartbeat stuttered and made it hard for her to breathe. *I've never wanted a woman as much as I wanted you that day.* Could that possibly be true? Even with that beautiful redhead vying for his attention? Had she underestimated her own powers of attraction to that extent? Apparently, she had.

'You made the right move,' Gianni told her disconcertingly. 'I wasn't looking for anything serious.'

'You were only twenty-two…why would you have been?'

'I had just come out of a long relationship, and I was enjoying my freedom that summer,' Gianni explained flatly, his lean, strong face shuttering.

Well, that was Gianni, Jo reflected helplessly. He shot her up to the sky one moment and dropped her down to below ground level the next. Sex appeal was something, but it wasn't worth quite as much if a woman knew from the outset that she wanted more. Gianni had got badly burned in that long relationship he had no wish to discuss. Was that why he only seemed to indulge in superficial affairs? Or was that too neat an explanation? After all, Gianni had always seemed to revel in his freedom. But she couldn't forget him saying that loving anyone just got you hurt.

'And the second time I asked you out, you were wearing a stupid hat with bunny ears and singing Christmas carols,' he reminded her.

'You do pick the worst moments,' Jo teased, her cheeks warming at the recollection. 'I was shocked.'

'You looked like an angel when you came inside to persuade my guests to contribute to your charity. I was hooked all over again.'

'So hooked that you forgot that your latest lover was sitting at the same table?' Jo scoffed with wide, wondering eyes. 'I knew you were together because I'd read it in the gossip columns.'

'Which just goes to show that you can't rely on gossip. She was with another man.'

'I got it wrong. I thought you were shameless.' Jo lifted her spoon to taste the lemon sorbet that had been brought to the table for dessert. It was delicious and refreshing.

'I am.' Gianni watched her licking the spoon, the pink tip of her tongue skimming over the metal, and every muscle in his long, lean body went rigid. She could wind him up like a clockwork toy, he acknowledged reluctantly.

He questioned that she even understood how the sex embargo had affected him. He already suspected that sex wasn't that important to her. She didn't understand how much he wanted her, and he didn't understand how she could be impervious to the electric tension between them. But even so, he knew that he wasn't about to quibble over her terms.

'*Every* member of your family phoned me while I was away,' Gianni told her over coffee.

Jo leant back in her seat and stared at him in horrified disbelief.

Helpless amusement slanted Gianni's expressive mouth. 'First, your grandmother to assure me that there wasn't a word of truth in that nasty woman's story.'

Jo cringed. 'And then?'

'Sybil breathing fire on your behalf. Enraged by my father's interference and stupidity and even madder than your grandmother about that article. Trixie was much more low-key and full of advice about the current full moon…and us needing to take advantage of it.' Brimming laughter dancing in his golden eyes as her gaze evaded his, Gianni grinned. 'I didn't like to tell her that there wasn't much chance of that…'

Jo's creamy skin had flamed pink. 'I'm sorry. I have embarrassing relatives. When did they phone you?'

'This morning. They love you very much and they are very loyal. If anything, I'm envious,' Gianni admitted.

'Where were you staying?' Jo finally asked. 'In a hotel?'

'No. An apartment in Rome. I've also been thinking…if you're in agreement, we will move on from here tomorrow and spend our week elsewhere,' Gianni continued. 'Coming to an isolated island wasn't the best idea. It may have worked for a normal honeymoon couple but a couple like us requires a little more outside stimulation.'

Jo nodded, although she was discomfited by the reminder that they were not a normal newly married couple. But then she couldn't have it every way, could she? And then she looked at him with a warmer gaze and accepted that she had forgiven him. He had apologised and for the very first time he had made the effort to explain himself. He was changing. He was *trying*. Didn't that mean that she could try to loosen up a little as well?

After eating, they walked down to the beach. Jo kicked off her sandals, lifted her long skirt and skipped along the edge of the surf. Like a child, Gianni thought as he watched her, relishing her lack of self-consciousness with him and her zest for life, not to mention her ability to forgive and forget one of his worst ever errors of judgement. Moonlight glimmered over her lovely face and his gaze centred on the luscious pout of her pink lips, laughter falling from her as the tide forced her to run back up onto the beach.

He closed long fingers round a slender

wrist and tugged her to him. For an instant, she remained static and then she shifted closer, lips parting in invitation, eyes luminous. Gianni caught her to him with possessive hands that curved to her hips.

For a timeless moment, Jo was still with anticipation and a growing sense of security. Gianni brought his mouth down on hers with a ravaging sweetness that dialled up the urgency already thrumming through her taut length. Her bra felt too tight for her breasts, the soft peaks firming to hard points and, breathless, she pulled back from him.

'Let's go back,' she muttered unevenly.

Gianni drew in a slow, deep breath and said nothing as they strolled back up the hill. He would not put her under any kind of pressure.

'Maybe we should consider taking advantage of that full moon Trixie mentioned,' Jo mumbled in a rush, terrified that she would lose her nerve as they entered the castle.

Without even glancing in Gianni's direction, Jo clattered upstairs to the bedroom they could have shared that first night. It was too late now for her to wish that they had. Had they consummated their marriage then he might well have appreciated that she could never have had an affair with Ralph behind anyone's back. Undressing, she lifted the filmy nightdress Sybil had given her, tossed it on the bathroom chair and stepped straight into the shower.

Grains of sand sprinkled the floor of the shower basin, and she suppressed an anxious sigh as insecurity threatened to overwhelm her. How could she possibly hope to meet Gianni's expectations? She wasn't the experienced woman he would assume she was. So, she had to be honest, enthusiastic, and quick to learn. That made her feel rather as if she were about to attend an evening class in an unfamiliar subject. Grimacing, she towelled herself dry and donned the nightie, which was rather more glam than her usual shorts and tee.

Running a brush through hair tangled by the sea breeze, she left the bedroom, only to freeze on the threshold at the sight of Gianni already sprawled across her bed, only a towel linked round his lean hips. Being Gianni, he looked even more enthralling half naked. His skin was the colour of bronze. She had not realised how muscular he was.

'What can I say? I'm keen,' he confided insouciantly as he watched the colour climb in her cheeks.

'Evidently,' Jo agreed, forcing her stiff legs forward and seating herself awkwardly on the edge of the bed.

'Why are you so serious?' Gianni chided, rising up on his knees to send his passionate mouth travelling very briefly over hers.

'Because this is serious for me,' Jo admitted as he closed his hands to her hips and pulled her up onto the mattress beside him. 'I haven't got naked with a guy before.'

His mobile black brows lifted. 'You can't mean that you're a virgin?'

Jo shrugged a stiff shoulder, her face burning. 'I didn't plan it this way. It just happened.'

'How did it just happen?' Gianni queried in surprise. 'You were at university. You must have had boyfriends?'

'A few, but nobody who made me want more from them. I just didn't meet the right guy and I wasn't interested in having sex purely for the sake of it.'

Gianni sighed. 'If only I had been as discriminating. I lost my virginity at fifteen to a girl a couple of years older. It was meaning-less. I don't deserve to be your first lover—'

'Oh, shall I go out and look for a more de-serving man?' Jo cut in playfully.

Gianni laughed. 'If I thought you meant that—'

'Well, if you make me discuss this any more I will,' she threatened.

'I've never been with a virgin before,' he confessed.

'Don't you think it's fortunate that at least *one* of us knows the score?'

Amusement lightened the darkness in his frowning gaze and he tumbled her into the pillows, smiling down at her with sud-den warmth. 'You always surprise me, Jojo. I never know what you're likely to do or say next.'

He kissed her until the blood was drum-ming in her veins and her heart was racing. His tongue twinned with hers and skimmed the sensitive interior of her mouth. A knot of excitement unlocked deep in her pelvis and her hips rose to his in an uncontrolla-ble wave. He was teaching her what wanting more entailed, and she was grateful that she had waited because she was convinced that, whatever else, Gianni would not give her a mediocre experience.

He reached beneath her to peel off the nightdress and as it caught there was a slight ripping sound that made him suppress a curse. 'I'll buy you another one,' he promised. 'Although you won't be wearing it much.'

'Forget it,' Jo told him, running her fingers through his black tousled hair as she sat up, determined not to be uncomfortable with her nakedness.

Gianni moulded a hand to a small pouting breast and pressed her flat again, an intent look narrowing his dark golden eyes. He let his mouth roam across her breasts and caught a pert pink nipple between his lips, pausing to suckle and savour the responsive bud, smiling as tiny sounds of appreciation escaped her parted lips. Tugging at the other swollen peak, he shifted his attention there, revelling in every sound he could wrench from her. He toyed and teased while her movements grew ever more frantic until the tiny little shudders racking her slender body strengthened and finally coalesced into a gasping cry of surprise and pleasure.

Rocked by that climax, Jo stared up at him,

her eyes sliding shut as he claimed her mouth in a hungry, driving kiss, and the tightness at the heart of her increased. She wanted more, she registered, she wanted more so much that her fingernails dug into the smooth skin of his back. For the first time, impatience was claiming her and she knew why he was taking his time and that it was for her benefit, rather than his own, but she was still tempted to urge him on.

Gianni traced a line with his mouth from her breasts down over her stomach and lower. When she froze, he kept going, ignoring the fingers flexing taut in his hair.

'I want you, *cara*. I want every bit of you that you are willing to share,' he growled.

Jo swallowed hard and rested back. He stroked the fluted pink lips between her thighs and she shifted, struggling not to jerk, a little quiver of powerful awareness running through her. He lowered his head and flicked his tongue across her clitoris and in seconds, as that electric sensation engulfed her to send a glittering arrow of heat into her pelvis, she was lost. The ache between her legs built and built, tightening muscles she had not known she had and increasing a

sensitivity that heightened by his every ca-
ress. He slid a finger into her hot, wet sheath
and then another, scissoring them to ready
her for him and she quivered as the excitement surged up and overflowed, sending her
careening into another climax.

Gianni slid over her and she felt him hot
and hard against her warm, damp entrance.
She trembled, struggling not to tense, eyes
wide at the sensations that gripped her as he
slowly sank into her. And then came a pinch
of discomfort followed by a sharp flash of
pain that took her by surprise and made her
cry out. Instantly he stopped.

'No, don't stop!' she gasped. 'Finish it!'

Her teeth gritted as he pushed deeper into
her untried body and then she felt him, hard
and urgent inside her, and she recognised
the strain etched into his darkly handsome
face as he fought to stay in control. The discomfort ebbed and he circled his lean hips
and withdrew before burying himself in her
again with a masculine groan of pleasure. A
wave of equally enjoyable response travelled
through Jo and she relaxed, her body sensu-
ally adapting to his rhythm.

'You feel so good,' Gianni confided in a ragged undertone.

Jo arched up to receive his next powerful thrust, excitement generating afresh, sparking in her tummy and blazing up to consume her as he increased his tempo. She lifted her hips up as he ground his body down into hers, setting off a chain reaction as the intensity of sensation clenched her every muscle tight. Hungry need gripped her as he slammed into her, control no longer his driving ambition, and ripples of delight rolled through her in an intoxicating wave.

Caught up in that wild exhilaration, she flew higher and higher, rejoicing in every very physical moment of that flight. Her body was humming and stretching and reaching, and then suddenly she was there where she most wanted to be, and a dizzying explosion of emotion and reaction engulfed her. Ecstasy flooded her, followed by convulsive spasms of intense sensation. In a world of her own, she was only dimly aware of Gianni's harsh groan of release and the jerk of his powerful body against her own.

'I've never had sex without a condom before,' Gianni murmured breathlessly into her tumbled hair. 'It felt wickedly erotic and forbidden.'

'Oh…' Jo responded and even finding her voice took effort when she was still drowning in the hazy aftermath of bliss. She felt weightless and drowsy.

'No, you're not allowed to go to sleep,' Gianni censured. 'You need to get in a bath to soak away your aches and pains.'

'I can't feel anything.'

'But you will tomorrow,' he assured her, springing out of the bed to stalk into the bathroom.

Still in a reverie, Jo lay listening to the water run. Gianni had exceeded her expectations and she didn't think it would be wise to tell him that. A sunny smile softened her mouth. No, she definitely wasn't about to tell him that.

A pair of hands slid beneath her and her eyes flew wide. 'What are you doing?' she exclaimed as she found herself in his arms.

Gianni slid her down gently into the warm water in the bath and she sat up and hugged her knees, feeling awkward and shy, which struck her as ridiculous in the circumstances.

'Do you do this for all the women you've been with?'

'Only wives,' Gianni declared deadpan. 'And you really *do* feel like my wife now, *cara*.'

He strode naked into the shower and she watched the bronzed silhouette of his lean, strong body through the water streaming down the glass, blinking rapidly as if that could somehow help to clear her foggy thoughts. She was happy, she thought in wonder, frowning at that unexpected development. Gianni's wife, a role she had never thought to fill and yet, here she was...

As she slid back into bed still feeling very sleepy, she turned her head on the pillow as Gianni joined her, her curiosity stirring. 'Can I ask what happened in that long relationship you had at university?'

'I prefer not to tell you. Talking about it only stirs up bad memories,' he told her bluntly, his lean, darkly handsome features taut and cool as ice.

Jo lost colour and flipped over to sleep with her back turned to him. He was under no obligation to tell her his every secret. Marriage didn't mean he had to bare his chest and tell all, she reminded herself. But even so, she reasoned, she had been forced to confide in him about Ralph and about her virginity and she felt as though she had no secrets left. Some reciprocal confidence and clarification from Gianni would have been welcome. She couldn't help but feel hurt by his lack of trust in her.

By the next morning, that shadow of anxious concern had faded. Jo winced when she got out of bed, the ache of soreness at the heart of her a surprise and a reminder of what they had shared. But she had no regrets, most particularly not when Gianni casually wrapped a towel round her as she emerged from the shower and then closed his arms round her. The effortless way he touched her and drew her close spoke volumes in the wake of his former reserve. Intimacy had brought down barriers that had made both of them stiff and uncomfortable. She smiled as he told her that, after breakfast, they were flying to the south of France. Without a doubt, there was a new ease between them. In time, she told herself firmly, as they forged stronger ties, Gianni's ability to trust her enough to talk to her would improve.

That afternoon, they arrived at the Provençal farmhouse, an idyllic old property built of stone with a weathered terracotta roof and a host of well-maintained ancillary buildings. It was surrounded by wheat and lavender fields and lush orchards of fruit trees. In the distance the snow-capped peaks of the mountains were visible.

A tiny man called Antoine greeted Gianni with great familiarity in French and Gianni had to interrupt his eager flood of conversation to introduce Jo.

'Antoine lives on site. He's a former chef and a fantastic cook. I used to come here every summer as a child with my mother. Sometimes, I was left here with a nanny while she returned to London for treatment,' he confided when he had taken her up to a big traditional bedroom. The bed linen was white, the windows were wide and a fat sheaf of purple-blue lavender in a vase scented the hot, still air. 'After she died, I didn't want to return because the memories of her here were too painful.'

'I'm surprised you brought us back,' Jo admitted.

'Enough time has passed now and it's a beautiful, tranquil place. We can relax here but we can also easily go out as well,' Gianni pointed out calmly. 'It feels good to be back under this roof.'

'I'm glad,' she told him gently.

Antoine served them a superb late lunch that included a tapenade starter and a sea bass and asparagus salad. The meal finished with home-made ice cream and fresh cherries. Replete and laughing at Antoine's suggestion that they might also enjoy some cake with their coffee, they sat chatting in the shade.

The next morning, Gianni took her into Villeneuve to explore the Saint-André gardens and the art exhibition in the abbot's palace. It was a peaceful place to wander, and Jo took countless photos for her grandmother's benefit. Liz Hamilton was the gardening enthusiast at Ladymead, and Jo knew that she would enjoy seeing the roses in full bloom, the beautiful pergola walk and the colourful mosaic of parterres and flowerbeds. The views from the terraces out over Avignon, the Alpilles and Mont Ventoux were spectacular.

An evening meal in a tiny exclusive restaurant completed the day.

Before they climbed back into the car, Gianni cupped his hands to her cheeks to keep her still and kissed her passionately. It was as though an electrical charge raced through her veins and the feel of his aroused body against hers only made her push closer to increase the connection.

'My word!' she exclaimed in the aftermath, rocked on her feet by how hot that single kiss had proved to be. The dull throb of desire between her thighs was instantaneous.

A grin slashed Gianni's mouth. 'You have the same effect on me.'

'I've recovered,' she confided shyly.

'Is that a fact, Signora Renzetti?' he teased.

Gianni's phone was buzzing when they entered the house.

'Go on up to bed and I'll follow you up,' he urged. 'I have to take this call.'

Her curiosity sparked and she glanced at his shuttered expression before going upstairs. She fell asleep long before Gianni joined her.

'Who was that on the phone last night? You were absolutely ages,' she complained when she wakened the next morning.

'It was Fiona, a close friend from my student days.'

'An ex?' Jo questioned.

Gianni compressed his lips. 'A connection,' he rephrased. 'She didn't receive our wedding invite, so the news that I was married came as a shock. I should've made the effort to phone her to tell her personally.'

Jo was annoyed that he had spent so long talking to another woman the night before. And what was the difference between an ex and a *'connection'*? Why was he being so secretive when it came to voicing simple facts? Furthermore, if the other woman weren't an ex, why would she be shocked by news of his marriage? And how was she supposed to feel when this was the *third* incident relating to another woman since their wedding, the third incident in the space of four days?

First there had been the hurt, jealous drunk at their wedding, then his fierce reluctance to discuss his past relationships. And now Fiona, the woman he had had to talk to in private. So, who was Fiona? A 'connection' or *the* actual ex-girlfriend who had hurt him when he was at university? Was it possible he was still in touch with his first serious love?

Stranger things happened, she acknowledged. In silence, Jo quietly fumed and fretted. How many other blasted women were likely to come out of the woodwork? She would have been less suspicious of Gianni had she not been aware of his womanising reputation prior to their marriage. As she saw it, that meant that Gianni required careful observation and handling, but she assured herself that she was too intelligent to openly parade her misgivings and make them a stumbling block in their relationship.

He stroked long caressing fingers down a slender thigh and Jo shifted and stretched like a sleepy cat. 'You missed a treat last night,' she told him out of sheer badness.

'I'm here now,' he pointed out.

'Too late!' Jo laughed as she slid out of bed with the dexterity of an eel escaping a net. 'Antoine promised to show me how to make croissants if I got up early enough.'

CHAPTER SEVEN

GIANNI WATCHED Jo vanish into the bathroom in a movement as sleek and fast as the flow of quicksilver and suppressed a curse.

He hadn't expected Jo to have a mercurial side, but she did. Yet she held his attention like a magnet. In addition, she enjoyed a depth of charm that could only impress him whether it was chattering to Antoine in her inept schoolgirl French or meticulously noting down the names of the roses she had captured in photos for her grandmother's benefit. She was gracious, kind, and thoughtful. In fact, his bride was a much more complex creature than he had initially assumed: disarmingly honest and chatty while at the same time contriving to be ridiculously mysterious. It disturbed Gianni that he very rarely guessed what was going on inside Jo's head before she spoke.

Gianni had gone when Jo returned to the bedroom to pull on shorts and a T-shirt ready for her baking lesson. Her generous mouth down curved and she scolded herself for that secret sense of disappointment. She refused to feel any more for Gianni than he felt for her. To get more deeply involved with him would only lead to her being hurt. He had spelt out the boundaries of their relationship and love didn't come into it.

He had work to catch up on, had mentioned that necessity the evening before. She was conscious that within days he would be facing the board meeting where he might still find himself voted out as CEO of Renzetti Inc. What would it do to their relationship if it turned out that their marriage had failed to change anything for the better? Then, she would be surplus to requirements, she reflected worriedly.

Gianni spent the morning working on his laptop and Jo strove to copy Antoine's slick skills in the kitchen with varying results. Gianni drank his espresso and accepted without comment a horribly misshapen croissant made by his wife's own fair hand. Later, having lost himself in work, he glanced out of the window and saw her weeding the shrubbery in the garden while Antoine cut the grass on the mower. He grinned. He could not think of a single woman he had ever been with who would have let him work undisturbed while quietly occupying herself with weeds.

He strolled out to talk to her. 'I'm finished for the day. Let's go out.'

'Give me another ten minutes and I'll have finished this,' she urged, wiping the perspiration from her brow. 'I hate leaving a job half done.'

'You look incredibly sexy,' he breathed in a husky undertone.

Jo studied him in wonderment. She was hot and dirty and sweaty. 'You can't be serious.'

'You really don't see yourself the way I do,' Gianni whispered, scanning the swell of her firm breasts above the camisole top, her tiny waist, and the length of her shapely bare legs. The damp sheen across her cheekbones merely enhanced her bright sapphire eyes. There was even a smudge of flour on her face from her baking activities earlier that day. 'Earthy and sexy…'

'I'll wash off the earth in the shower,' she declared.

'But not the sexiness,' he quipped with a slow-burning smile.

That magnetic smile did something to her. It lit her up inside like a torch and she had never been more conscious of her body as she climbed the stairs. *He* did that to her, let her connect to the sensual side of her nature, the one she was only just learning about. She looked at him and she wanted him. It was that simple. It had *always* been that simple, she acknowledged belatedly. Without her ever admitting the fact even to herself, for years Gianni had figured as her perfect male fantasy figure. And with Gianni as her ideal, was it any wonder that she had never deemed another man worthy of serious interest? That awareness embarrassed her.

Even though she had never seriously believed that she would ever be with Gianni, even though she knew that their lifestyles were incompatible, she had cherished that secret fantasy of the bad-boy billionaire who could charge her up with the most wicked hunger with one electrifyingly casual smile. It shook her that she could have been so unaware of what went on inside her own head. Sybil had guessed. *'You've always wanted him,'* her great-aunt had said bluntly when Jo had told her about Gianni's proposal. Sybil had had no doubt whatsoever that Jo would marry Gianni.

She hadn't married Gianni solely for her family's benefit or for Ladymead, Jo appreciated guiltily. She had fallen back on convenient excuses to protect her pride. She had wanted him for herself. She had had a photo of Gianni on a polo horse on the inside of the door of her school locker. He had sent it to her when his team won a big match. But she hadn't let the rest of the sixth form see it because she hadn't been willing to share it or him.

As she stripped off her grimy clothes she looked at herself in the bathroom mirror and wasn't surprised that she looked hot and flushed. The lies she had told herself to save face!

She stepped into the shower. As she emerged from the glass cubicle again, a muffled squeal was wrenched from her when she realised that she was no longer alone.

Gianni held out a towel and wrapped it round her. 'You hadn't locked the door. I thought it was all right to join you,' he murmured soothingly.

'You're not the only one of us who needs to remember that we're a couple,' Jo admitted with pink cheeks as she lifted another towel to dry her hair. 'And couples share…stuff.'

'Like beds,' Gianni agreed with dark eyes alight with merriment.

'You came in here with an ulterior motive,' Jo registered.

'Guilty as charged,' Gianni responded equably. 'The thought of my very beautiful wife in the shower naked and alone was too much for me.'

Jo flipped back her damp hair and rested her fingertip against his full lower lip, noting the shadow of stubble that had appeared there since morning. 'How many times have you said that to a woman?'

'You're the only wife I've ever had,' Gianni told her with strong satisfaction as he eased her closer, brushing away the towel so that it dropped to the floor.

Every line of his lean, powerful physique was pressed to her naked body. She felt the urgent thrust of his erection. She slid her hand down his chest and allowed her fingers to trace the hard, ready length of him and he shuddered against her in response. She found his responsiveness to that slight advance incredibly hot.

With a stifled groan of surrender, Gianni lifted her up fully into his arms and carried her into the bedroom to tumble her down on the bed.

'I should have dried my hair!' Jo exclaimed.

Gianni laughed out loud. 'Forget your hair, *cara*. Recognise your priorities here,' he urged.

Jo flung her head back and surveyed him appreciatively. 'Are you saying that you expect to be my priority?'

Gianni's stunning dark golden eyes gleamed as he peeled off his tee shirt, revealing his strong shoulders and the solid wall of his muscular chest. 'What do you think?' he traded as he toed off his shoes and began to unzip his trousers.

'I think that, yes, you *expect* to be my first and only priority,' Jo murmured with amusement. 'But I know that you don't appreciate anything that comes to you too easily. You like a challenge. It intrigues you.'

Gianni discarded his boxers and came down on the bed, reaching for her in almost the same movement, his hungry urgency providing another lift to her confidence.

'I want you so much,' he breathed raggedly.

'I like that,' Jo told him truthfully. 'I like to be needed.'

'Right now, I need you like I need air to breathe,' Gianni growled.

He nipped along the fullness of her lower lip, teasing her into opening her mouth before taking rampant advantage by sliding his tongue against hers and making her shiver with reaction, her whole body suddenly so sensitive it was ridiculous.

He pushed her knees back and she felt him brush against her damp heat. Hooking her legs over his shoulders, he rose over her. Disconcerted, she gazed up at him in feverish anticipation, locked to the smouldering gold of his eyes. He sank into her hard and fast, filling the emptiness, stretching her to fullness until she didn't know where he began and she ended. The pleasure came in an intense surge that made her inner muscles clench.

'You feel divine,' Gianni groaned, snaking his hips to pull out of her clinging flesh only to surge in again with even greater vitality. And so it began, a passionate assault on her senses as he plunged into her again and again and she bucked and arched beneath him as the excitement between them built. A frantic ferocious need climbed inside her. Her hands raked through his hair, over his shoulders and down his back. Her heart was racing, her skin damp with perspiration and then she reached a climax in a great rush of sensation that triggered an intoxicating explosion of reaction. Gianni jerked and shuddered with an uninhibited shout of satisfaction and then they both slumped, drained by the pleasure still rippling through their connected bodies.

'Was I too rough?' he whispered into her hair.

'No, I liked it…like that,' she framed unevenly, still trying to catch her breath. 'But I'm glad Antoine is still out on the mower because he would have heard us if he'd been indoors.'

Gianni burst out laughing as he released her from his weight and rolled over, only to curve her round to face him again. 'Only you would think of that,' he said appreciatively.

'I think we expended so much energy that we've almost dried your hair.'

'It'll be like a haystack after that,' Jo forecast without much concern because she knew she would be getting back in the shower to wash it again. 'Gran used to say I had hair like my mother and it had a will and a life of its own.'

'You never talk about your mother.'

'I have no memory of her at all. I have photos of her, but I only know her through what others have told me about her,' Jo confided. 'It's all second-hand and some of it is likely just conjecture.'

'Tell me about her,' Gianni urged.

'She was quite independent. She married a man who was a lot older when she was twenty and it was against my grandparents' wishes. Unfortunately, the marriage didn't last and she wouldn't come home to the family after the divorce. I kind of understand that,' Jo admitted wryly. 'Her brother, Abraham, was the star on the home front because he was an up-and-coming businessman and Grandpa's big hope for the future. He was always being held up to her as the act to follow. There wasn't really room for her to be herself there and she had an office job in London, lots of friends and a good social life.'

'When did she get pregnant with you?'

'A few years after the divorce. My grand-parents didn't know until after I was born and she brought me back for a visit. They offered to keep me during the week so that she could work and she agreed, saying she would spend week-ends with us at Ladymead. Six months later, she died in a train crash on her way to visit.'

'It's tragic that both your grandmother's children died before her. It's possible that I could have enquiries made to see if we could establish who your father is…if you were in-terested?'

Jo gave him a rueful smile. 'Thanks, but no, thanks. I have all the family I need. Sybil thinks my father may possibly have been a married man and a colleague of my mother's. I think I'll let sleeping dogs lie. I can live with not knowing.'

Gianni pulled her closer and curved an arm round her. 'I felt I should offer.'

'It's a kind idea but I'm happy as I am,' she told him truthfully, loving the easy affection with which he held her close even though she reckoned it was virtually meaningless to a man who had already decided she only had a shelf life of five years' duration. A minimum of five years for her as wife could also mean Gianni's maximum, she reasoned, wondering why she hadn't seen that possibility before.

'Hi, this is Jo,' the voice declared brightly. 'I'm sorry I can't come to the phone right now. Please leave a message and I'll get back to you later...'

Gianni almost threw his phone at the wall in frustration. How many times had he listened to Jo's voicemail? He had told her what the time difference was and she had still tried to call him back when he was asleep! He had barely spoken to his wife in two long weeks. He had asked her to accompany him to New York for the all-important board meeting that would decide his future. Jo, however, had cited the many workers starting repairs at Ladymead and her need to help her family to move out into their temporary home in the village and he had grudgingly given way.

He strode down the gilded corridor in the penthouse that his mother had once furnished like the Palace of Versailles. Glimmers of that theatrical magnificence still lingered in the elaborate walls and ceilings, but Fiona had made a clean sweep of all the fussy furniture and had installed modern pieces.

Gianni was in a rage. Fresh from the board meeting that had lacerated his hopes and expectations, he was in very bad form. While his position as CEO of Renzetti Inc had been confirmed, the board had insisted on reviewing his status in three months' time. Gianni, who had made multimillion-dollar profits for the business, was *on probation*. Nobody had employed that provocative term but that deferred decision had still gone down with Gianni like a lead balloon. He had wanted certainty and certainty wasn't on offer. Consequently, it seemed to him that he had got married for nothing. Certainly, his marriage hadn't paid off!

What was even worse in his opinion was that no sooner had they returned home than Jo seemed to have become perpetually unavailable. Her driving motivation seemed to be finding a million things to do other than simply being *his* wife. And he wanted Jo around more. He wanted her with him. Why shouldn't he feel like that when they were a couple?

He had brought forward his flight home. It infuriated him not to be able to speak to

Jo. He had wanted to tell her about the board meeting, had known that she would instantly make him feel better about that contentious decision. Unlike him, she had a way with words. But Jo, it seemed, had little room for him in her busy itinerary. They were still in the first month of their marriage but Jo was more interested in her family's needs, not to mention organising the co-ordination of the complex repairs on Ladymead and the housing of her pets. He had little doubt that she was also still loyally meeting her duties at the church and for her various charities! Only Gianni seemed to have drawn the short straw.

That same morning, Jo screened a yawn as she endeavoured to keep the joiners and the roofers from each other's throats as they quarrelled about who had arrived first and who therefore had the right to clear everyone else out and start work unimpeded. Jo was already stressed by the fact that her grandmother had tripped over a rug and hurt her ankle and Sybil had had to take the older woman to the local A & E for treatment. Trixie was fairly useless in a crisis, prone to panic attacks and absolutely hopeless at handling grumpy men. While Jo suggested staggered access to the foreman as a means of keeping the peace between the various work teams, she pushed back the hard hat, which was hot on such a warm day, and longed for the fresh air and the chance to shed her fluorescent high-vis jacket. The council health and safety representative had insisted that everyone who crossed the threshold of the house had to wear protective gear even though the real work hadn't started yet.

Jo checked her watch as the workmen reached agreement and she left them to it because she had to help prepare the church hall for the summer jumble sale. Her grandmother had volunteered and Jo felt duty-bound to cover for her absence. She wondered where Gianni was and what he was doing. Most of all, she wanted to know how that board meeting had gone and he hadn't called her yet.

Shedding her safety gear with relief in the front garden, she headed back to Belvedere where Duffy, on his perch in the orangery, greeted her with a biblical quote. "'In the world you will have tribulation…'"

'Thanks, Duffy. Just the cheery word I needed,' Jo jibed.

The house her family would be using until Ladymead was liveable again was too small for a parrot with a giant noisy personality and Gianni had agreed that the bird could stay with them.

'Have you time for lunch, Jo?' Abigail asked as she passed back through the hall.

'Give me five minutes. I'm all dusty and I need to change first,' Jo confided as she hurried up the stairs.

At the top of the staircase, she felt suddenly dizzy and grabbed onto the balustrade to stay upright. She had broken out in a cold sweat as well. Breathing in slow and deep, she wondered if she had been racing around too much in the heat, although she hadn't had much choice about that after her grandmother's fall. Trixie had been in hysterics and she had had to rush over there. And she still hadn't remembered to thank Gianni for having a gate cut in the wall between Ladymead and Belvedere, so that she could easily move between the properties without taking a car out onto the road.

She grabbed the first cool dress that met her eyes in her dressing room, an old favourite that still had plenty of wear in it even if Gianni had suggested that she should now be dumping her older clothes and utilising the designer garments she had worn on their short honeymoon.

A dreamy look momentarily crept across Jo's face. Those few short days in Provence had been magical. She had never felt closer to another human being than she had felt to Gianni, but she didn't kid herself that it had been the same way for him. Gianni had buckets of charm and she was quite sure that most women responded to him as she had. He was very passionate, but she didn't count sex as an advantage. Gianni liked sex and he found her attractive. She refused to believe that that made her anything special in his eyes. So, here she was, talking herself down again, trying not to get too emotional about stuff.

Unfortunately, without even trying, Gianni could hurt her feelings as well. Out of sight seemed to be out of mind when Gianni was involved. He had only phoned her a couple of times since he had departed and her chatty texts had gone unanswered apart from the very first when he had texted back,

What are you telling me this stuff for? Do I care about scaffolders who have gone missing?

She hadn't felt that that was much of a joke, but then he was in the midst of work at a tense time and she had clearly irritated him, so she had simply ignored that response and had kept on texting, striving not to be too thin-skinned and to keep up a cheerful front.

Downstairs, Abigail had a salad waiting for her in the dining room. Jo ate with appetite. She had risen soon after first light when Trixie had phoned about her grandmother's accident and she had missed out on breakfast when she'd gone to help. Thanking the housekeeper, she left the house and walked to the church through the grounds, enjoying that pleasant amble along the shaded walk below the trees.

Gianni's helicopter landed on the helipad at Belvedere. He was tired and unshaven and he would have enjoyed a shower, but he was even more determined to run Jo to earth… and ground her, possibly *for ever*. He strode into the grand house to be greeted by Abigail.

'Where's Jo?' he asked lightly.

'I'm afraid I don't know. She was here for lunch but, to be honest, she doesn't spend much time here. She's probably next door organising the tradesmen. Mrs Renzetti is a tireless worker,' she said admiringly.

Gianni's lips compressed. 'She is,' he

agreed as he turned on his heel and headed back out again.

He strode through the arched gate he had had constructed and walked into the Ladymead front garden. He didn't stop to admire his foresight. In fact, just about then, he thought it had been crazy of him to facilitate her visits to her family and make her more accessible to others. When was she planning to make time for *him*? He had texted her to tell her that he was coming home. He had expected either a response or to find her waiting for him. To receive neither had only angered him more.

He found Sybil in the barn feeding her motley collection of animals.

'Oh, she's at the church for the jumble sale,' she told him brightly.

McTavish whimpered behind a metal mesh gate, penned in and clearly hating it.

'Why's he locked up?' Gianni enquired in surprise.

'He couldn't be trusted with the tradesmen.'

'Let him out,' Gianni urged.

'Are you sure? I thought he hated you too.'

'No, we're making progress,' Gianni insisted as he opened the gate and McTavish emerged, visibly thought about attacking him and then stilled with a bewildered expression on his face. 'Come on, we'll go find your mistress.'

A jumble sale. His wife was helping with a jumble sale. He had vaguely assumed Jo did only hands-off stuff like fixing flowers in the church and of course she sang solos in the choir on special occasions. It was infuriating to credit that even a jumble sale was more important than he was on Jo's terms.

He strode into the garage and climbed into his sports car. He was about to reclaim his wife. McTavish barked at him. 'Forgot about you.' Gianni sighed, opening the passenger door, trying not to wince as the Scottie sprang into the car and sat down, flexing his claws on the pristine leather upholstery.

He drove round to the church by the road. He had no doubt that Jo had walked, ignoring the fact that he had a brand-new four-by-four sitting ready for her use. She shunned personal gifts if she could get away with it, yet she accepted that he cover the heavy expenditure of the repairs to Ladymead. Annoyance snaked through Gianni and his dark golden eyes flashed with ire.

He strode into the church hall, which was a hive of industry. Women were rushing about setting up stalls and unpacking bags and boxes. He saw Jo and then he saw nobody else. He was so intent on reaching her that he almost tripped over the priest and was then forced to pause and make gracious small talk when he was anything but in the mood for it. He watched Jo over the elderly man's shoulder. What on earth was she wearing? Some sort of shapeless cotton shroud the colour of grass? Or the colour of grass stains? He couldn't decide. But even that ugly garment couldn't stifle her luminosity, the gold of her hair and the jewelled perfection of her eyes against her pale skin. A hunger as unstoppable as his temper lanced through Gianni and he thoroughly resented that surge of lust.

Jo looked up from the box she was unpacking and saw Gianni and everything, literally *everything* just fell away from her as if someone had waved a magic wand. He stalked through the crowd looking very much like a Greek god, an exquisitely tailored black pinstripe suit sheathing broad shoulders, lean hips and long powerful legs. A red shirt and silver-grey tie bucked the conventional vibe he had utilised for the board meeting. The cut male lines of his perfect features were breathtakingly spectacular even with a heavy cloud of stubble darkening his skin. Jo stared and a helpless stab of yearning was followed by a far more earthy inner clench that made her flush and press her thighs together. For a split second, she couldn't believe she was married to him or that the same man could possibly have declared that she was a cut above him. He was her perfect ten and he was *home*. Only a split second from rushing forward to grab him and rush him back to Belvedere, she encountered his eyes and she froze.

His dark golden eyes were scorching hot, his lean, darkly handsome face taut and hard. She frowned because he was clearly angry. What the heck had happened to put him in such a mood? My word, was her first thought, had the board of directors ousted him from his position?

Gianni leant over the stall to say, 'Why aren't you at home?'

Jo blinked. 'Oh, my goodness,' she whispered. 'Why did nobody tell me that I'd been spirited back in time to the nineteen fifties?'

CHAPTER EIGHT

GIANNI'S SHIMMERING EYES flamed like torches in receipt of that comeback. 'I texted you to tell you that I was on my way back—'

Jo dug her phone out of her pocket, her palm damp. 'No, you didn't,' she began and then she realised that her phone was as dead as a dodo because it had run out of charge. 'Oh, dear.'

'Is that all you've got to say?'

'Let's go outside to have this conversation,' Jo urged, moving out from behind the stall. 'I don't want anyone overhearing us and I can only give you five minutes.'

'Five minutes?' Gianni seethed, only half under his breath.

'I have to take care of the stall. There's no one else to do it.' Jo lengthened her steps to walk outside as fast as possible. The back of the church hall housed the bins and the occasional smoker, but it was at that moment quiet and empty. 'I'm sorry I didn't get your text. I forgot to charge my phone.'

'If I can't even reach you on the phone,' Gianni shot at her, 'what sort of marriage is this?'

'Obviously not a marriage that meets your expectations,' Jo conceded with stiff reluctance, wounded by that question. 'You're doing that not-listening thing that you do when you get angry. Take a deep breath, count to ten, whatever works for you.'

At that advice, Gianni's gaze flared with incredulity. A moment later, he stepped hastily out of the way as an elderly woman trod past him to plunge a bag into a bin, exchanged a cheery word with Jo about the queue forming at the front of the hall, and went back indoors.

'Your phone battery is past it. If you were actually *using* the new phone I gave you…'

'Gianni…the phone you gave me has diamonds all over it,' she reminded him in a pained whisper. 'It's very extravagant.'

Gianni shrugged a broad shoulder in dismissal. 'You reject everything I give you. The phone, the car, the clothes, but when it comes to Ladymead, you take it *all*.'

'Stop scoring points. It's not like that, you know it's not,' Jo begged. 'Please, just tell me how the board meeting went.'

Gianni stepped back, shoulders squaring, mouth taut, bright narrowed eyes grim. 'I'm still CEO but they're planning to review the situation again in three months.'

'Oh, no, I know that must make you feel like you're still on trial!' Jo exclaimed in dismay and immediate sympathy, moving closer to stroke his arm in a consoling gesture. 'I'm so sorry, Gianni.'

'I feel like I'm getting absolutely nothing out of our marriage,' Gianni spelt out in a harsh undertone as she stepped back from him again. 'You're never there for me.'

Jo stared at him in a panic. 'Don't say that!'

'Why not? It's the truth.' Gianni was not in the mood to give any quarter. 'You could have been in New York *with* me. Instead, you put your family and Ladymead, even your blasted pets before me! You're my wife. I should take precedence.'

'I think that sounds very old-fashioned,' Jo protested even as guilt and regret burned through her like a stream of lava because she had not realised that he resented her choices quite so much, had indeed assumed that he would be far too much in demand to miss her. For her, however, the days of his absence had run one into another in a mad blur as every day had thrown up new complications at Ladymead or fresh family challenges. 'I'll start using the new phone.'

'Too little, too late,' Gianni breathed in a tone of finality. 'A month into our marriage, I can't accept that it's extraordinary that I should expect more of your time.'

That criticism hit Jo hard. At that moment, it seemed to her that everyone in her life was expecting more from her and that, one way or another, she was short-changing or disappointing all of them. Sharp anxiety engulfed her. The days weren't long enough to cover all that she had to do, and now Gianni was home with every right to expect her attention and some cruel fate had ensured she was unavailable.

'Perhaps not. Gianni... I have to go inside now and finish setting up the stall,' she muttered apologetically, her sapphire eyes clinging to his lean, strong features in vain search of some understanding of her predicament. 'I'll be home in a couple of hours.'

'As you wish…' Gianni turned on his heel.

'We'll continue this back home,' Jo pointed out. 'Let's hope I don't lose my temper as well.'

'I haven't lost my temper,' Gianni countered with quiet dignified assurance, for he had been careful about containing it. 'Nor have I said one word that I regret.'

Jo went back into the hall and finished unpacking. The scrum of shoppers kept her from thinking too much about the argument. She felt crushed by Gianni's dissatisfaction though. He deemed her a complete failure in the wife stakes. Clearly, he had wanted her with him in New York. She had got that decision badly wrong. Furthermore, she should be using the new phone and the new car and wearing the clothes. He was spending a fortune on her family home and she wasn't quibbling about that, so why was she refusing to utilise his generous gifts? That was petty and thoughtless of her. He saw it as a form of rejection and she had offended him.

'"Give every man thy ear, but few thy voice,"' Duffy warned as Gianni walked through the orangery and strode outside, drinking in the fresh air after the hours of travel and strife. The parrot's Shakespeare quote only made Gianni groan.

Jo would never have agreed to marry him had he not promised to repair Ladymead. That was the crux of the problem, he reasoned tautly. Strip all the other stuff away and what was he left with?

'She married me for my money,' he reminded himself, thinking that his expectations had been too high, if not out of order.

Just inside the doorway, Duffy trilled in delight and began singing his song about money making the world go around, pacing to the beat along his perch.

'But she wasn't a gold-digger.' Gianni sighed, accepting that essential truth that was an obstacle that stretched like a mountain range between them.

Even so, if Jo didn't have time for him or their marriage, he had a very practical solution to the problem. He needed to hire a project manager to free his wife from the onerous duties of overseeing the work being done on the money pit. That was simple, straightforward, a first step in the right direction, he told himself ruefully. He would organise that transfer of labour immediately and free Jo from the responsibility. In addition, he would organise a break for them on the yacht because they had had a very brief honeymoon, and marriage, he was beginning to appreciate, required a lot more effort and time input than any casual affair.

Jo walked back to Belvedere with McTavish and Fairy at her heels. She was deeply troubled. Gianni had treated her unfairly. He had not looked at his own behaviour. He had kept every one of his secrets, locking her out, keeping her at a distance and refusing to give her his trust. Yet she had told him everything about herself without reservation. He had allowed his father to insult her with his allegations about Ralph only the day after their wedding and he had not had enough faith in her to defend her. That had hurt and damaged her ability to trust him.

And whether he liked it or not, Jo had a responsibility towards her family. Gianni didn't really have a family beyond a father he barely spoke to and her as his new wife, so how could he understand her position? Jo had gladly taken charge for Sybil at Ladymead after her grandmother's fall and had stepped in at the jumble sale because her family would have done the same thing for her. Such things happened and had to be dealt with sensibly.

'I'll bring you tea. Mr Renzetti is on the terrace,' Abigail told her cheerfully.

'"Though she be but little, she is fierce,"' quoted Duffy randomly as she petted him as much as he would allow, which wasn't much. He had never been a touchy-feely bird although he was happy to sit on a family member's shoulder if invited.

'Whatever,' she muttered, bracing herself and walking out onto the terrace.

'Finally, you're here,' Gianni purred with more than a hint of sarcasm as he lounged back against the wall that separated the terrace from the lawn that stretched right to the edge of the natural woodland.

Gianni had changed since she had last seen him at the church hall. He had shaved and exchanged his suit for designer jeans and a casual shirt the rich green of a pistachio nut. He looked stunning. That shade brought out the bronze of his skin and the darkness of his hair. And his sun-kissed skin accentuated the smouldering dark gold of his gorgeous eyes. Her husband, only he really truly wasn't hers, Jo reflected unhappily. He was a husband on temporary loan and that time element of a five-year maximum could well relate to his lack of trust in her and in other women.

She was to stay his wife for a minimum of five years but was that not really a clue that five years was the longest Gianni could see their marriage lasting? Or even wanted it to last? Certainly, that time limit was not something that Jo could manage to forget. Sadly, she couldn't argue about that limit either, she acknowledged, not when she had agreed to that contract, her only thought being the saving of her family home. Unfortunately, once that five-year period had been mentioned, she had only been able to view their marriage as a very transitory affair, which Gianni could already see ending. And that aspect, when she had been doing nothing to avoid a pregnancy, could not give Jo any peace of mind.

Abigail bustled out with a tray of tea. Gianni waved away the offer of tea as a refreshment in favour of the whiskey glass in his hand, but Jo was thirsty and she poured herself a cup.

'I have some things to say,' Jo announced then, her lovely face pale, her eyes shadowed with tiredness, her expression unusually serious. 'Sybil intended to look after the work at Ladymead, but my grandmother had a fall and Sybil had to cry off to take her to A & E for treatment. She's okay. It's only a sprain. But that's why I was over there this morning. The jumble sale was something my grandmother had volunteered to do and I took care of it for her this afternoon.'

'Jo…' Gianni murmured tautly.

Jo set down her cup and saucer and stood tall. 'No, let me speak first. You didn't once *tell* me that you wanted me to accompany you to New York. My family moved out of their home this week and they needed my help. There's a big gap in trust between us, Gianni.'

Gianni angled his dark head back, eyes glinting in the sunshine as he frowned. 'I disagree.'

'If that's true, why can't you tell me who the love of your life was at university?' she asked levelly. 'Why can't you talk freely about Fiona? Those are simple questions that people in a relationship would normally ask and have answered. That you refuse tells me that you don't trust me…and that makes it hard for me to trust you as well. You are, after all, the man who stood back and let his father accuse me and question me about false allegations made against me.'

'Federico wants a private meeting with you to apologise for his behaviour,' Gianni interposed. 'He phoned me about it over a week ago. He knows he was in the wrong and that he shouldn't have interfered. We'd have heard about that tabloid article soon enough through your family.'

'None of that changes the fact that *you* didn't have faith in me.'

His smouldering gaze narrowed, his strong bone structure clenching hard at that blunt reminder. 'I thought we had already laid *that* business to rest.'

Colour flamed over her cheekbones. 'Forgiving you doesn't mean I forget how you acted,' Jo pointed out defensively, her voice rising involuntarily. 'Or how you're acting now. As if I've let you down…as if I have no right to be loyal to my own family! As if sometimes life doesn't force you to roll with the punches because you have to do the right thing. My loyalties were torn between you and them! Why can't you understand that?'

Gianni set down his glass and reached for her, his hands dropping down on her shoulders. 'Jo—'

Jo broke angrily free of his hold. 'No! Right now, I'm going for a nap to make up for my very early morning start today and then I'm going to see my grandmother, where I will stay for dinner. I'll see you later. Maybe by the time I return you'll have started trying to see things from my side and not just your own!'

Slammed by that criticism, Gianni made no attempt to hold her back and he watched her stalk back into the house, proving that she was as close to losing her temper and screaming at him as he had ever seen her.

Bemused by that raging comeback from peaceful Jo, of all people, Gianni groaned out loud. Should he follow her? Or wait, let her have a break and allow the dust to settle? The truth was that he didn't honestly know what to do because he had never been in a relationship long enough to have arguments, unless he counted his time with Fliss, and Fliss had

never once argued with him about anything.
So, that somewhat unreal experience was of
no help whatsoever.

He had been in a bad mood when he flew
home, he conceded grudgingly. It galled him
to admit that he had been unreasonable, possibly even selfish. But he had been. He had
missed her in New York. He had wanted her
by his side. Only he hadn't been prepared to
admit that to himself. Getting mentally attached to Jo had never been part of his plan.
How naïve had he been to believe that he
could marry a woman without making the
smallest adjustment to his new lifestyle?

All his adult life, Gianni had believed that he
had to have complete control over his emotions
to protect himself and, until Jo had appeared in
the church on their wedding day, he had fully
believed that he had achieved that feat. But little by little, Jo had infiltrated his life on every
level. Sexual attraction was no longer Jo's main
appeal. He expelled his breath slowly, wondering why he had such a powerful need for her
presence, her company, her validation.

Jo raced upstairs, walked to the master bedroom and stripped off her dress, which she

now loathed. She had seen how Gianni looked at that dress and she knew it hadn't passed muster. It could go to a charity shop. From now on she would wear her new wardrobe. She slid into the comfortable bed with a sigh. She would have made more effort if she had known that Gianni was coming home that afternoon. There she had been wearing a comfortable but shapeless dress and wearing no make-up. She winced.

Gianni was accustomed to the company of beautiful, well-groomed women, many of whom would be willing to invite him into bed regardless of the wedding ring on his finger. Why did she care? What difference would it have made? Had she looked more alluring, would he have scooped her up in his arms and kissed her breathless? Jo rolled her eyes. No, he had been too annoyed with her. She muffled a yawn and, tucking her cheek into the pillow, closed her heavy eyes. Why, oh, why was she so extraordinarily tired?

Gianni studied Jo intently while she slept. Once again, she hadn't been looking after herself, he decided worriedly. She had blue shadows beneath her eyes and there was a hint of frailty to her fine bone structure. Abigail had admitted that Jo didn't eat very much and usually ate on the run, always rushing from point A to point B to cover her various obligations. And he had made her feel bad. A trip in the yacht would do her the world of good.

Jo felt much better when she awakened and stepped straight into the shower to freshen up. She donned a flowing blue sundress with a designer label and slipped on a toning cardigan to cover the cooler evening temperature. Keys clutched in her hand, she climbed into the brand-new four-by-four Gianni had gifted her to drive it for the first time and turned it down the manicured drive slowly before, gathering confidence, she headed for the village and her family's temporary home.

One step in the door of the low-ceilinged house, she learned that Gianni had already visited and had brought flowers to her grandmother. He had also, apparently, reiterated his suggestion that her relatives simply move in with them at Belvedere for the duration of the work being done at Ladymead. Her grandmother had politely refused, once again voicing her conviction that newly-weds needed their own space.

Liz Hamilton looked reasonably well after her ordeal, her bandaged foot resting on a stool. But she looked exhausted and every year of her age. Jo's heart clenched tight. Since her sister was out of action, Trixie had cooked and dinner was a vegetarian feast.

'Gianni is worried about you,' Sybil remarked. 'He thinks you look very tired.'

'I'm fine. We've all been run off our feet with the move this week,' Jo protested. 'He fusses.'

'And so he should. He's your husband,' her grandmother said staunchly. 'It's his job to look out for you.'

'Is everything good with you?' Sybil asked, her keen gaze probing Jo's strained smile.

'Everything's marvellous,' Jo swore.

After telling that lie, Jo couldn't face going inside Belvedere when she got home. That would mean dealing with the fallout from her bitter exchange with Gianni. It was a pleasant light evening and she decided to walk down to the lake instead of going directly indoors.

The lake path was shaded by trees, and she was glad of her cardigan because it was cool. The waning light left long stretches of the lake in darkness and it was a little eerie. In daylight it was beautiful though, a tranquil expanse of water surrounded by trees and leafy water plants. A duck fluttered up out of the undergrowth at her approach and she flinched and gasped. Her invasion caused a noisy exodus of birds and a bunch of them surged across the path and into the water. She sat down on the bench her grandfather had installed for his fishing.

The faint thud of steps on the grassy path made her look up as a long, tall shadow blocked her view of the lake. 'Gianni?' she wheezed in surprise.

'I saw you walk down in this direction and wondered where you were going. You never come down here,' he murmured with a frown. 'Yet when you think about it, this is virtually where we started. Not the best of memories but the experience created a bizarre link between us, didn't it?'

Her stomach hollowed as she remembered him walking into the lake that day and she looked up at him with wide, troubled eyes.

'You never betrayed me. You never told my

secret,' Gianni mused reflectively. 'It makes me wonder why I've been so reluctant to trust you.'

'I didn't really understand what I'd seen you do until I was a bit older. I just thought you were being foolish.'

'I *was* foolish…and out of my mind with grief,' Gianni sliced in heavily. 'My mother provided the only warmth and softness in my life and I couldn't face the future without her. I was angry and bitter that I didn't get to be with her at the end. When I walked into the lake, I didn't want to come out of it again. I was very intense, an all-or-nothing teenager.'

'Yes,' Jo agreed ruefully. 'After you rescued me, you looked at me like you hated me because I'd stopped you in your tracks.'

'I would have drowned if it had not been for you. What on earth possessed you to go into the lake to try to reach me?'

Jo tensed, for she had often asked herself that same question. 'It was instinctive. I felt so desperately sorry for you because you'd lost your mum. I was a good swimmer, only unfortunately I didn't have time to think about what I was doing. I only knew that you walking into the lake like that was very dangerous and I wanted to stop you.'

'So, you got into the water yourself and almost drowned before I contrived to fish you out.' Gianni groaned as he crouched down fluidly in front of her, his stunning dark golden eyes alight with emotion. 'Jo, you have too much heart…it was a crazy but very brave thing for a little girl to do.'

'I wasn't expecting the weeds and I got all tangled up and then I panicked,' Jo recalled hoarsely.

'You made such a commotion in the water that I realised I wasn't alone and struck out to see what was happening. I saw you sinking below the surface, that red jacket you were wearing ballooning up round you.'

'You saved my life,' she whispered.

'But you saved mine as well,' Gianni pointed out levelly, closing a lean hand over her knotted fingers. 'It must've been fate… How else can you explain us being together now?'

Jo lifted her head, faint amusement dancing in her eyes. 'Careful, Gianni…you almost sound romantic.'

'Why did you never tell anyone about what you saw me do that day?' he asked wryly.

'I didn't want to get you into trouble. I mean,

I knew what you did was stupid, but I found your father scary back then and I assumed you'd be punished even though you'd lost your mother.' Jo sighed. 'It was just easier all round to let everybody believe that you'd seen me in the water and gone in to rescue me.'

'The last thing I wanted that day was to be christened a hero when I didn't deserve the accolades.'

'But you did deserve them because you *did* save me,' Jo contended gently. 'We kind of saved each other.'

'Yet, right now, it feels like I've blown everything apart with you,' he breathed tautly. 'That's not what I intended when I married you. I did want to make a go of this.'

'We both do,' she conceded gently as he vaulted upright and pulled her up with him. 'So, *talk*…fill in all the blanks for me.'

'It was first love,' Gianni explained flatly as he walked her back in the direction of the house. 'I don't know if Felicity—Fliss—was the love of my life exactly, because I was only nineteen and in my second year at uni when I met her and her sister. Fliss and Fiona were identical twins. She was studying art history.

I fell madly in love with her. We hung around in a group.'

'Most of us do at university,' she chipped in, disconcerted to learn that the Fiona he was still in touch with was his ex-girlfriend's identical twin sister. 'I bet you were really popular because you're clever, rich and sporty.'

'I did have a lot of friends,' he conceded.

'What was Fliss like?'

'She was tall with long dark curly hair, obsessed with art, always dragging me off to exhibitions. I faked my interest. I'm not particularly into art,' he confided. 'She liked to cook, she liked to feel that she was looking after me. She thought I worked too hard, but then I had Federico at home, questioning even a hint of a lower grade in any subject.'

Jo breathed in deep, afraid to interrupt him. 'How long were you together?'

'Two years. But only a couple of months after we met, Fliss started finding bruises in random places. She went to the doctor. Blood tests were done. Leukaemia was diagnosed,' Gianni continued in a curt undertone. 'She went straight into chemotherapy. The doctors were hoping for a remission, but the treatment didn't make her any better, although the sessions probably extended her life. She got weaker and sicker, and in the end she died.'

Jo was utterly appalled by what he was telling her in that flat, unemotional voice. Only a few years after his mother had passed away after her long struggle with cancer, Gianni had found himself in love with a very sick girl.

'I was devastated,' Gianni admitted gruffly. 'Fiona helped to get me through it. She was very close to Fliss and was with us from the beginning. I wanted them to move into my apartment with me, but Fliss didn't want that. They didn't have any other family. Their uncle had raised them and he died shortly before they started university.'

'I'm so sorry, Gianni. I can understand why you didn't want to talk about her now,' Jo said uncomfortably because her throat was thick with tears. She was thinking about Gianni, whose childhood had been staged against the daunting backdrop of his mother's illness, falling in love with a girl who had also become ill and ultimately died. She realised now why he had told her at Ralph's funeral that falling in love only got you hurt, because the only two people he had loved in life had died and left him behind. Her heart broke for him and her eyes stung and she had to breathe in deep to stay in control.

'Fiona is still in your life, though,' she remarked carefully.

'She's like the sister I never had,' Gianni said warmly. 'I set her up in business after we finished university and she's gone from strength to strength, one of the best investments I've ever made. She renovates and decorates houses with real flair. She's made quite a name for herself abroad.'

'I look forward to meeting her some time,' Jo replied.

'Are you satisfied now that I've told you everything?' Gianni enquired as he walked her upstairs.

'It wasn't a matter of needing to know so much as a need to know that you trusted me enough to tell me,' Jo explained tautly. 'Don't make a secret of things just because you would prefer to avoid talking about them.'

In their bedroom, Gianni slowly turned her round to face him. His dark golden eyes were very serious and his hands flexed on her slim shoulders. 'Stay in touch with me when I'm away. Send me your silly texts telling me what Duffy said or how McTavish got frightened off by a fox. I like hearing from you. That connection is important to me, *cara*.'

'I do not send silly texts,' Jo declared with amusement.

'You do and they lighten my day.'

'Then what about the text about the missing scaffolders that irritated the hell out of you?' she dared.

Gianni groaned. 'Once again, my apologies. Federico and my uncles were with me complaining about profit margins in this new company we've acquired.' He fell silent, recognising that she was smiling and that he was forgiven.

In relief, Gianni bent his dark head and brushed his lips very gently across hers before sliding his tongue against hers in a hungry exploratory foray. 'What do you think of early nights?'

Her slender body quivering against the hard muscularity of his, Jo struggled to catch her breath. 'One would be very welcome right now,' she muttered unevenly.

Gianni scooped her up into his arms and tumbled her down on the bed. 'I like this dress but it's coming off,' he warned her.

'We're going away for a week on the yacht tomorrow and sailing round the Greek islands.'

'But I can't leave—'

'Yes, you can, it's all organised,' he overruled as he stood back and peeled off his shirt. 'Sybil will take over supervising at Ladymead. Trixie's shop is closed at present, so she'll be able to keep your grandmother company until her ankle heals.'

Involuntarily deprived of speech, Jo stared up at him.

'I discussed it all with your family while you were sleeping. I want you all to myself,' Gianni admitted with a slashing smile. 'The honeymoon part two.'

Jo sat up to lift her dress over her head and discard it before coiling back against the pillows like an embryo temptress with a glint in her bright eyes. All of a sudden the world felt as though it was full of infinite possibilities. 'I may pack my wedding dress and those lace gloves. I seem to remember making you a promise.'

Gianni flat-out grinned, lean muscles flexing as he came down on the bed and shifted over her, sliding between her slender thighs. Smouldering dark golden eyes glittering, he was all sensual heat as he strung a line of kisses across her collarbone and arrowed off into the sensitive skin of her neck to press his mouth there, making her hips arch up and a little gasp escape her.

Jo laced her fingers into his tousled black hair. 'I want you,' she said for the first time ever. 'I missed you.'

'I'm not sure you had time. According to Sybil you've been racing around like the Energizer bunny.'

Jo tugged his head up. 'Very funny. I kept busy because you weren't here,' she told him.

Gianni gave her a smile that was pure invitation and shifted lazily against her, the sensual spell he could cast holding her fast as her heart rate climbed. 'I'm here now...ready, waiting and very willing...'

CHAPTER NINE

Jo BOUNCED HER sandalled feet to the annoying pop song playing in her head. She had heard it in a restaurant on Corfu and still couldn't get it out of her head.

Ten days had passed since they had left for a tour of the Greek islands. A dreamy smile tilted her lips. Island-hopping round the Greek islands had been enormous fun. There had been picnics in secluded bays and once on a rugged hillside where a herd of goats had tried to steal Gianni's lunch. Just thinking about it, she laughed again. They had visited Little Venice on Mykonos and ended their day there dining by the shore where Gianni had given her another ring, a diamond hoop that had shone brighter than the stars above them. A magical trip to the volcanic island of Santorini had followed and they had walked hand in hand up the steep streets, taking advantage of the most spectacular sea views. The nights were hot and very passionate, she recalled abstractedly, emerging from her reverie to wonder why she was sitting on the edge of the bath when she had already showered.

And then reality stole back and she paled and remembered that she was anxiously awaiting the result of the pregnancy test she had done. She hadn't thought it was possible to fall pregnant so quickly but then her period had failed to arrive while they were abroad and she had begun to worry. After all, now that she was finally thinking about that momentous decision to try to get pregnant from the very start of their marriage, she was guiltily regretting it. She hadn't really thought through the consequences of an early pregnancy when their marriage was still very much in the honeymoon phase. It would alter so much between them.

She had no doubt that Gianni would be pleased that she had conceived because he had made that same decision with her. Sadly, neither of them had devoted much time and thought to that life-changing choice. How much did Gianni know about pregnant women? That they got big? That they shouldn't drink alcohol? That they had to take extra care of themselves and got tired more easily? Wouldn't he find all those restrictions a drag? Mightn't he find her larger body a bit of a passion-killer?

Finally, Jo checked her watch and reached for the wand. Well, she was pregnant, no doubt about that. A bubble of happy satisfaction broke through her insecurities. Gianni's baby, she thought dreamily, *their* baby. Maybe a little boy, maybe a little girl, she didn't much care which, only that her child be healthy. It had happened. She wouldn't be surprised to learn that Trixie had cast some crazy fertility spell on them at the full moon. There was nothing the Hamilton women loved more than a baby in the family. *I'm going to be someone's mum,* she thought dizzily, absolutely blown away by the idea.

She would tell Gianni when she was ready to tell him. Just at that moment she wanted to hug her precious secret to herself for a little while. In the meantime, she would see her doctor, have herself all checked out and present Gianni with the complete package. Why? She suspected that her pregnancy would make Gianni inclined to fuss over her every move and she wanted to be in a position of superior medical knowledge.

Jo went downstairs for breakfast in a pensive mood. She was surprised to find Gianni, superbly sleek and sophisticated in a tailored navy suit and an unusually conventional white shirt, still seated at the table reading the *Financial Times*. 'I thought you had an early flight,' she remarked.

'The meeting was moved back and I rescheduled. I'm leaving in five minutes,' he warned her briskly, all switched into business mode, which made her want to smile.

Madre di Dio, that beauty of hers could light up the room, Gianni conceded, shaken by the thought, particularly when it came directly after his decision to leave her peacefully sleeping earlier when, in truth, he had wanted her company. Their relationship had shifted from a business deal to a level of complexity that stunned him. He told himself he didn't need to think about it, that the closer they got, the better and more successful their marriage would be. But there was no denying that what they had was very far removed from what he had originally envisaged. As a rule, he skipped late travelling and stayed in London overnight, but Belvedere had developed an allure that had nothing to do with bricks and mortar and Gianni knew that he wouldn't be spending the night anywhere but with his wife.

Jo helped herself to tea and toast and then wondered if she should be eating more protein and, when Abigail came in to check on them, surprised the older woman by asking for scrambled egg.

'*Madonna mia,*' Gianni swore in sudden impatience. 'I meant to tell you last night but I forgot. Fiona arrived last night.'

Jo tensed. 'Fiona?' she queried. 'I didn't realise she was coming here so soon—'

'She wouldn't have been if this were purely social. I hired her services,' Gianni told her, his satisfaction over that decision patent. 'She'll take care of everything at Ladymead for us. It's win-win for everyone. She'll put Ladymead in some glossy-magazine spread when it's all finished and it'll be great PR for her and attract more business.'

Jo was so stunned by that quickly delivered speech that her jaw literally dropped.

Gianni slanted his charismatic grin, even white teeth visible, dark golden eyes glittering with amusement. 'I've finally found out what it takes to silence you...one little surprise—'

Jo relocated her tongue. 'I would hardly call Fiona a *little* surprise,' she murmured stiffly. 'Have you already arranged this with her?'

Gianni smiled even wider. 'I'm very efficient,' he told her smoothly. 'Our estate manager informed me earlier that she picked up the keys for the gate lodge yesterday, so she'll already have moved in.'

'She's going to be living in the gate lodge?' Jo gasped in astonishment.

'With the job she's going to be doing for us, she needs to have somewhere to stay nearby. Why not the lodge? Until we have a head gardener hired, the property is sitting vacant. I would have offered her a room here but we need our privacy,' Gianni advanced cheerfully. 'It wouldn't kill you to say thank you at this point.'

An expectant silence spread from his side of the table.

'*Thank you?*' Jo repeated loudly, still reeling in shock from his announcements. 'Are you kidding me?'

Gianni raised a brow as he set his espresso cup down. 'Why would I be kidding you, *cara*? Fiona is the answer to all our prayers. You'll get to be a lady of leisure and I'll get to see a lot more of you. Sybil will be able to return to her rescue animals with a clean conscience. It will suit everyone.'

'But you didn't consult me!' Jo exclaimed rawly. 'You didn't even *discuss* it with me!'

'I organised it for you that day you were at the jumble sale and I meant to raise the subject with you but I forgot about it again,' Gianni told her with a distracted air as he checked his watch and sprang upright. 'Sorry, time for me to depart.'

His long stride got him as far as the threshold of the dining room when he turned back to her. 'I arranged for you to meet Fiona for coffee at eleven today at that new place in the village…what do you call it?'

With difficulty, Jo snatched in oxygen to breathe. 'As You Like It?'

'I thought it would be less formal for a first meeting and that you might not want to invite her here until you get to know her better,' Gianni advanced, in the same helpful *I'm only thinking of you* tone.

Jo was keeping a very tight hold on her temper. She wanted to scream at him but she wouldn't let herself when he was about to leave. 'Didn't it cross your mind that Sybil and I might *want* to take care of Ladymead ourselves?'

Gianni shrugged a broad shoulder. 'Well, it's too late now. Fiona turned down another job to come here at short notice. She's doing us a favour. Why are you making such heavy weather of this? I assumed you'd be grateful for Fiona's help.'

As he moved on into the hall, Jo flew upright and followed him, her cheeks flushed, her eyes bright. 'Ladymead is my home and you went beyond your remit when you organised Fiona without consulting me or my family about it,' she told him frankly.

'First of all, *this* is your home now.' Gianni frowned, taken aback by her attitude when his only thought had been to release her from the burden of overseeing repairs in a dirty, dusty environment. 'You don't get to be consulted unless you're an expert…and you're not an expert in any field relating to that building, aside from its history. I make the major decisions about Ladymead because I'm paying for the work being done,' he framed with succinct bite. 'And I'll have to pay more if any mistakes are made, particularly the kind of mistakes that might fall foul of the rules to protect a listed building and would have to be rectified before the authorities will certify the work.'

And with that unsympathetic and cutting statement delivered, Gianni swung on his heel without another word and strode off for the helipad.

Jo's hands knotted into fists. He *forgot* to tell her about hiring Fiona? Chance would be a fine thing! Gianni wasn't that innocent. He had been determined to release her from the demands of Ladymead while the repairs were being carried out. Maybe he thought she was going to sit at Belvedere all day sewing a fine seam or however that stupid phrase went! What did he think that she was planning to do with herself all day? Ever since she'd left uni, she had been running Ladymead, taking care of the accounts, keeping everyone happy, dealing with every little problem.

But maybe that phase of her life was over now that she had Gianni, Belvedere and his other homes to consider, she reflected uncertainly. Was that possible? Did she need to do a rethink about her life too? How dared he speak to her like that though! Yes, she knew very well that he was financing all the work, but he hadn't had to throw it in her face like that, had he? She could have said in much the same vein, 'Yes, I know you're paying for it. Isn't that why I married you?'

Ironically, Gianni would have hit the roof at that taunt. It wasn't something he ever mentioned. He had pretty much bought her with Ladymead, but he didn't like to be reminded of that hard fact. It seemed that he now wanted her to be the woman of leisure he assumed would suit his needs best, always available, always on call, as easy as his past undemanding lovers, there for him the instant he snapped his fingers. Her even white teeth gritted and she said a very unladylike word under her breath.

And now she was stuck with Fiona, whether she liked it or not! Fiona, who was like his sister, she reminded herself grimly. Well, he had accepted her family and she had to accept his, even if Fiona was only an honorary member. She tackled her scrambled egg and fresh toast with a murmur of thanks and a lack of appetite she concealed. Being at odds with Gianni stressed her out. Had she been unreasonable? She called Sybil for a second opinion and Sybil's annoyance at being summarily replaced without warning reassured her as to her own wounded feelings.

'Gianni thought he was doing me a favour. He seemed to be expecting us all to be delighted,' Jo proffered apologetically.

'And a woman you've never met being installed in a house at the foot of your driveway? What on earth was he thinking?' her great-aunt fumed on her niece's behalf.

'The truth is that he doesn't think a lot about things from my point of view.' Jo sighed, deciding not to mention the prearranged coffee date, news of which would probably send Sybil into orbit. Talk about Gianni being high-handed! Taking over? Moving her around on his own mental chessboard as if she had no will or wishes of her own and no other life. He was utterly ignoring the truth that she liked to be busy and active as much as he did.

'He needs to learn to communicate…and fast.'

'Agreed. It's quite challenging.'

'His father is too, although if you give Federico a good dressing-down, he does eventually get the message,' Sybil informed her tellingly.

'I thought I had you to thank for that apology of his,' Jo admitted with sudden amusement. 'He was very embarrassed. He's getting rather more human than he used to be. Are you seeing him socially? I don't like to ask if you're *dating.*'

'Good heavens, no!' Sybil gasped. 'He's trying but he's not there yet, particularly with that stupid stunt he pulled with you and Gianni when he crashed your honeymoon! He'll have to up his game a lot before I give him another chance.'

But Federico Renzetti obviously went for strong women, Jo reflected thoughtfully as she went upstairs to go through her wardrobe, trying to pick an outfit that would do for a visit to her doctor and, afterwards, the coffee date with Fiona. Dress up, she decided, unable to imagine Gianni having such high regard for a woman who wasn't elegant, at the very least. She donned a lightweight pair of trousers and a matching top in a light summery print.

Her doctor confirmed her pregnancy and wished her well, sending her off with a prescription for vitamins and a lot of useful advice. Jo walked into the coffee shop and ordered tea, instead of her usual coffee, and took a seat at a table in the window.

A woman pulled up outside in a sports car. She was eye-catching with her mane of black curls tumbling down to her slim shoulders, perfect long tanned legs displayed in a short white skirt and a clinging white sleeveless top that hugged her curves. She strolled into the coffee shop, snapped her fingers at the startled barista and ordered an espresso. Every eye was on her because she looked like a celebrity. Her sunglasses were on top of her head, her sheer confidence showed, and she was, not to put too fine a point on it, gorgeous. She had big sparkling dark eyes, a glowing complexion and luscious red-tinted lips.

'You're Jo. I saw the wedding photo online.

I'm Fiona Myles. You must have some courage taking on Gianni,' she remarked with a mocking smile as she approached Jo's table.

'You think so?' Jo laughed, thinking that that wasn't the nicest way to greet a new acquaintance.

'I *know* so,' Fiona replied seriously. 'He doesn't wear monogamy well.'

Jo shrugged, not knowing quite how to answer that leading comment. 'That hasn't been my experience.'

'Initially I was simply so shocked that Gianni had got *married*,' Fiona admitted in a tone of disbelief.

'You're not alone,' Jo said lightly.

As the obedient barista delivered Fiona's coffee to the table, she smiled and thanked her. 'I can't wait to see Ladymead. I adore old houses,' she declared.

'Would you like an official tour tomorrow morning…about ten?' Jo asked cheerfully.

'That would be good. I want to get started asap,' Fiona told her. 'Gianni has never been patient. In fact, in all the years that I've known him, I've realised that when he wants something done, he wants it done yesterday. Some people don't understand that about him.'

And once again, Jo ignored the challenge, the underwritten hint that Fiona knew Gianni far better than Jo ever could. 'Are you comfortable in the gate lodge?'

'Very,' Fiona assured her as she hefted a fat file onto the table and thrust it across to Jo. 'My most recent commissions. Now, tell me about the repairs that are ongoing.'

Jo was happy to do so while warning that her grandmother and her sisters were planning to move back in as soon as the electric was back on.

'I'll advise them to stay where they are,' Fiona responded. 'It's not a good idea to try living on a work site and it could even be dangerous.'

'I agree,' Jo said. 'But my relatives are stubborn.'

Jo leafed through the file, noting that Fiona had done a lot of renovation work and interior design but that none of her projects had related to historical buildings. She chewed at her lower lip and deliberately admired the image of an opulent bedroom to be polite. In truth she thought it contrived to be both flashy and bland. Fiona's style was in no way suited to Ladymead's ancient quirky charm and eccentric layout. But she said nothing. Gianni's sister, she reminded herself firmly, determined to make the best of their association and handle the brunette with tact. She was disconcerted, though, by Fiona's very personal remarks about Gianni. That attitude didn't quite strike the right familial note to Jo's ears. In fact, Fiona's stance put Jo more in mind of a woman hostile to Gianni's marriage and his wife, a woman who was possessive of him because, for whatever reason, she had long considered him hers. Or possibly her late sister's?

'I'll see you tomorrow, then.' Fiona waved and departed.

Jo's phone rang as she was walking back into Belvedere.

'How did you get on with Fiona?' Gianni asked.

'I didn't expect to hear from you this morning again, not after the tone of your departure,' Jo confided in a tone of censure.

'I'm sorry. I'm too used to everyone agreeing with me and if they don't I tend to steamroller over them,' Gianni admitted tautly. 'I shouldn't have said that about the money.'

'Why not? You didn't say one word that

wasn't the truth, even if I didn't like what you said,' Jo conceded, striving to match his honesty. 'Fiona? The jury's still out on that one. She made a couple of snarky comments, one being that you're not monogamous. But I suspect that she wouldn't have warmed up to any woman you married, so I'll give her a pass on this occasion. Perhaps she was looking at me and resenting me and the position I was in because she lost her sister and wishes *she* were your wife. I want to be fair.'

'She shouldn't have said that to you.' Gianni warmed her heart by conceding that point. 'Fiona doesn't have many female friends. She's more a man's woman.'

'Didn't need you to tell me that, Gianni.' Jo chuckled, reckoning the short skirt and clingy sex-bomb top had told her that loud and clear. 'But if she's good at her job I'll do my best to get on with her.'

'You're being generous. I'll be late back tonight,' he warned her. 'But I'd still like to see you.'

'Oh, by the way, before I forget again,' Jo added, 'thank you for that gate through to Ladymead. It makes it so much easier to visit.'

'You see, I do get most things right,' Gianni drawled rather smugly, and she didn't pick him up on it.

Early evening, Jo went for a walk with the dogs and, on the way back, heard gales of laughter coming from Ladymead. Wondering who on earth was there when the house was empty and the workers finished for the day, she walked through the arched gate and into the front garden. There she was disconcerted to find Sybil, Trixie and Fiona Myles seated at the stone garden table with glasses and a couple of empty wine bottles discarded on the grass beside them.

'We're waiting for a taxi,' Sybil announced with very careful diction.

Trixie tried to say something and then caught her sister's eyes and just giggled like a schoolgirl.

'Fiona called in and we brought her over to see the house,' Sybil volunteered as a horn honked in the drive and the older woman stood up. 'That'll be us,' she said and grabbed Trixie's hand to urge her upright. 'Time to go home, Trix.'

Fiona beamed at Jo. 'I'm sure you're surprised to see me here, but Gianni told me where your family lived and I dropped in to see them.'

'It's good that you've met all of us now.'

'Would you like a drink?' Fiona asked.

Jo walked towards the house. 'A glass of water will do me. Alcohol would send me to sleep.' Not to mention her conviction that drinking with the client's family was as unprofessional as visiting the property without the owner present. Tact, she reminded herself, *tact*. She had to switch the water on and then run off the first discoloured gush for several minutes before she could risk satisfying her thirst and by then Fiona had joined her.

'I've got so many ideas for this kitchen,' the brunette told her, leaning back against the table and continuing to drink her wine.

'My grandmother will have her own ideas, too,' Jo warned her.

'Oh, don't you cook?'

'Not if I can help it.' Jo laughed. 'And I'm not living here at present.'

'Fliss was a fabulous cook.'

'We all have our different talents,' Jo responded evenly. 'I wasn't taught to cook. When I was home from school, my grandfather was too busy teaching me how to keep the accounts and how to nurse along our very basic plumbing system in winter.'

'Excuse me, I've got something to get out of the car.' Fiona turned on her high heels and staggered ever so slightly. 'When I come back, I'll tell you my ideas for the Great Hall. Get rid of those moth-eaten screens and the space will be transformed. More space... more light!'

Jo rolled her eyes, because the medieval hand-carved screens were a special feature of the house.

'Let's go back outside. It's gloomy and dusty in here,' Fiona complained, a large photo album in one hand and another bottle of wine in the other. 'Where's the corkscrew gone?'

'It's outside on the table.' Jo was thinking that, by the uncoordinated way Fiona was moving, she had already had more than enough to drink.

Outside again, Fiona pressed the photo album across the table. 'I brought this for you to have a look at...it's from when Gianni and my sister were together.'

'Thanks, but no. I would feel like I was prying,' Jo said truthfully, sipping her lukewarm water while Fiona poured herself a fresh glass of wine and frowned when Jo shook her head. 'And we can't move the screens.'

'I'll talk to Gianni about it,' Fiona cut in, her mouth tight as she pushed the photo album aside, annoyed that Jo had refused to look at it.

'No point talking to him about it.'

'Gianni is very open to my ideas.'

'But the local authorities wouldn't be. The screens are protected by law. They're listed. We're not allowed to remove them,' Jo explained gently.

Fiona grimaced. 'But they're ugly. I'm sure Gianni would agree with me.'

'It really doesn't matter if he does or not. It's *my* house, Fiona.'

'Surely, it's your grandmother's house?'

'No, my grandfather left it to me because I'm the last Hamilton in the family. My grandmother, naturally, has the right to live here as long as she likes,' Jo explained. 'I'm your client.'

'*Gianni's* my client.' Fiona's hostility was no longer hidden. 'He hired me, he pays me, *he* has the last word!' she asserted sharply.

'I'm afraid that I have the last word when it

comes to Ladymead,' Jo countered as gently as she could because she didn't want to make the other woman even angrier.

'I wouldn't take that for granted,' Fiona responded in an acid tone. 'You do your five years with Gianni and, in return, he fixes up this house. It's a business arrangement and he's only married to you in the first place because of that stupid scandal in the newspapers!'

Jo went white and literally stopped breathing for several timeless seconds. The private information that Fiona was flinging in her face was only known to a handful of people: Gianni, the lawyers involved and Jo. Even Sybil didn't know about that five-year clause. That Fiona was aware of that fact cut Jo to the bone with angry chagrin because she knew that the most likely explanation was that Gianni had told Fiona the exact circumstances of his marriage. And why on earth would he do that? Didn't he understand the concept of discretion?

'Perhaps you should lay off the wine,' Jo murmured tautly. 'My marriage is none of your business. I'm your client, not your target. I think you should return to the lodge now and have a good night's sleep.'

'Gianni would be much better off with someone like me!' Fiona flung at her, the words slurring. 'He should've been with Fliss but that wasn't to be, and he and I are very close friends indeed.'

'I'm sure you are.' Jo was determined not to get into an argument as she stood up. 'Goodnight, Fiona. Do you still want to do that tour of the house tomorrow morning?'

'Of course not!' the brunette snapped brittlely. 'I won't stand for you treating me like this!'

Jo made no response but inside herself she felt like glass that had been trodden on and smashed to pieces. She did not want to accept that Gianni had put her in a position where she could be humiliated. Their marital agreement was supposed to be private, not something he shared with a woman like Fiona, who only wanted to put her down. As the brunette stalked away, Jo turned back. 'Tell me…do you resent my existence on your sister's behalf? Or on your own?'

'Gianni said he'd never marry after Fliss died!' Fiona slung at her accusingly, but Jo recognised Fiona's jealousy. It was personal. Maybe Fiona had hoped that Gianni would turn to her after her sister died. It hadn't happened, but Fiona had still cherished hope as long as he was single. His marriage, business arrangement or not, had seriously rattled the brunette.

'People change.' Jo didn't say it, but Gianni had matured from the heartbroken young man he had once been. Her heart was hammering with stress inside her chest and she found it impossible to swallow as she walked back towards Belvedere.

Fiona was half in love with Gianni. It took one to know one, Jo acknowledged heavily. She was so hurt now because she was no longer detached from Gianni in *any* way. Not only was she pregnant, but also in love with him. When had that happened? Or had that development been inevitable? He was the boy she had craved as a teenager, the young man she had fallen passionately in love with. Her restive fingers touched the bouquet pendant at her throat. Gianni knew how to touch her heart. He knew what to say, what to do to entrance a woman. Jo had been a pushover, a complete pushover from the evening she had put on her wedding dress again for his benefit and when he had inched off each lace glove with deft fingers her heart had been hammering so hard she had been scared it would burst.

'I will never forget how beautiful you looked on our wedding day,' he had told her on the yacht with one of his flashing smiles. 'Everyone always says that a bride is beautiful, but you looked spectacular.'

And he had meant it, every word of it. She had practically flung herself at him afterwards, but she did not regret the wedding night that they had spent apart. She honestly believed that Gianni would not have appreciated her in the same way had she got into bed with him that first night.

In a pensive mood, she walked back home, wondering wearily if there would be repercussions for her decision to stand up to Fiona Myles. Gianni's friend and honorary sister. Well, what was done was done and she wasn't about to beat herself up for defending her own corner, and Gianni had questions to answer as well, she reflected ruefully.

A long lazy bath relaxed her. She dried her damp hair and picked an elegant wrap and a short silk pyjama set from her packed drawers. When she told Gianni about the baby, she wanted to look good. She was on the stairs when she heard the helicopter overhead and she smiled.

Gianni's fast, impatient stride carried him indoors before he even saw Jo at the foot of the stairs, wearing something fluttery, feminine and blue that bared her perfect legs. With supreme effort, he mastered the immediate surge of hunger that made his heart race and the fit of his trousers tight. He strode forward, smouldering dark golden eyes glittering below the thick canopy of his lashes.

'What on earth did you say or do to Fiona?' he demanded hoarsely.

CHAPTER TEN

JO FROZE, WARM COLOUR washing up her throat into her cheeks as she tried to think how to answer that leading question.

Gianni released his breath in a hiss of annoyance and said levelly, 'Fiona was in hysterics when she phoned me, and I had a hell of a job getting her off the phone again. I'm just asking what happened to set her off in drama-queen mode.'

Jo was in no mood to discuss Fiona Myles. 'Well, possibly *I* got annoyed.'

'You don't get annoyed…not the way I do and other less controlled people do,' Gianni rebutted with confidence.

Jo leant back against the carved pillar that adorned the foot of the stairs, unaware that that position pushed her bare breasts against the silk top she wore and showed a tantalising few inches of her smooth inner thigh. 'In this case, I got annoyed,' she confided.

'Why?' Gianni was attempting to look directly at her without being distracted by that very sensual pose that affected him in all sorts of inappropriate ways. The timing was all wrong, he thought regretfully.

'You see,' Jo continued, 'Fiona quoted the exact terms of our marriage contract to me—'

His ebony brows drew together. 'That's impossible!' he insisted. 'Only you and I and the lawyers are aware of that agreement.'

'Naturally, I assumed that *you* had told her,' Jo replied, but she was impressed by his air of incredulous surprise.

'*Madonna mia*, I'm not on those kinds of terms with her. I would only have discussed that with someone I was intimate with— I don't just mean sexually when I use that word, I mean someone to whom I speak without reservation,' he clarified. 'And you are the only person in my world who has *ever* known me on such intimate terms.'

Jo laughed, startling him, startling herself. 'I was just fixing to have the most massive row with you,' she explained unevenly. 'And you've cut the ground from under my feet.'

Gianni was still frowning. 'Fiona could only have found out from a leak at the lawyer's office. It'll have to be investigated. I expect the strictest confidentiality in my private business,' he declared with a grimace, digging out his phone.

'Phone them tomorrow…it's almost one in the morning!' Jo pointed out. 'So, can I take it from that that you have never been intimate in any way with Fiona?'

'Of course not,' Gianni asserted very drily. 'Surely she didn't give you that impression?'

Jo shrugged a slight shoulder. 'To be honest, I didn't know what to make of her. I think she feels more than friendly towards you and certainly not sisterly. Possessive, jealous. She had had too much to drink and it loosened her tongue. I can't be sorry for that. I couldn't have worked with her. She has no respect for boundaries and she likes to make sarky remarks.' She sighed. 'She even produced a photo album that contained pictures of you and her sister together. I mean, *why* would she do something like that to me?'

'That's weird. Did you look at the album?'

'No, I did not. I know it's all in the past but I didn't want to see you with another woman…' Not looking all loving and caring, as she was sure he did in such photos with his lost love. It would only have underlined what *she* didn't have with Gianni.

'I would have felt the same about seeing photos of you with another man,' Gianni told her, looking thoughtful.

'"Speak low if you speak love,"' Duffy quoted, perching on a plant pedestal.

'It's bedtime, Duffy,' Jo told him, extending her shoulder for him to clamber on board. She put him in his giant cage and covered it. 'Night, night.'

'"Love looks not with the eyes, but with the mind,"' the parrot recited.

'Spot on, Duffy,' Gianni remarked. 'Do we have to give him back? I like him.'

'We'll see,' Jo said as they returned to the hall. 'Abigail left supper for you. I'll put on the kettle.'

'I'm not hungry...well, not for food,' Gianni admitted rather abruptly. 'You look ravishing, *cara*.'

'I thought we were about to argue about Fiona.'

'No. I'm embarrassed that I trusted her and she behaved so badly. She lied about what you had said to her. Fortunately, I know you well enough to know that she was lying,' Gianni murmured, his mouth twisting. 'She's a drama queen and she likes to be the centre of attention and, of course, there was no chance of her taking pole position with you here.'

'I'm not a drama queen. I don't even like being the centre of attention,' Jo began defensively.

'No, but you are the indisputable queen of Ladymead *and* Belvedere,' Gianni informed her with a charismatic smile. 'Queen of my heart as well, if there is such an expression…'

Jo lowered her lashes, wondering what he meant by that. 'Not something I ever expected you to say.'

'Not something that I ever thought I would say,' Gianni confided, bending slightly to lift her up into his arms. 'If I have to put you down before we get up both flights, at least give me points for trying,' he urged.

Airborne without warning, Jo gazed up at him in astonishment. They reached the first landing. Gianni grinned and carried her up the second flight with a perceptible look of achievement. 'Let's forget about Fiona and the lawyers' office leak and all the other stuff that clutters up our days,' he suggested. 'I rushed home instead of staying in London tonight because I wanted to be with you.'

Jo's bright smile illuminated her flushed features. 'Truly?'

'Yes. I am truly hooked on you,' Gianni told her without hesitation.

'I like the sound of that.' Jo slid off her wrap and lay down on the bed.

'Sadly, I only realised what was amiss with me this morning. I'd just been ignoring my feelings. I've always done that and then those feelings just knocked me flat when I looked at you,' Gianni confessed ruefully. 'I don't know when I started loving you. I only know it happened and I can't picture my life without you now. You crept up on me. It started with desire and ended with me wanting to keep you for life. For ever and ever and all that jazz...'

'Done,' Jo murmured. 'It's a new deal. You don't ever get to look at another woman again. You only get to look at me. You only get to love me. And it'll be the exact same for me because I'm very possessive of you and I will not share you with anyone except our children. And this is where I have news to share with you.'

'You love me too?' Gianni cast his jacket and tie aside and came up on the bed to join her, ignoring the reference to her news. 'How did that happen when I put my feet in it every chance I got?'

'Well, it started with a crush when you were a teenager.'

'Are you serious?' Raw amusement danced in Gianni's dark eyes.

'Do you remember sending me a signed photo of you playing polo?'

He nodded slowly.

'I stuck it on the inside of the door on my school locker and never shared it with anyone, which was really mean of me because you had a lot of admirers when I was in sixth form,' Jo confided.

'I was such a flirt,' Gianni admitted.

Jo nodded agreement. 'But you'll practise not being flirtatious now that you're married,' she pointed out.

'So there will be rules. I expected that,' Gianni volunteered with a grin, gazing down at her with a new tenderness in his gaze. '*Madonna mia*... I love you so much. I couldn't wait to get here tonight, *cara*.'

'That five-year clause in our agreement. What was that all about?' Jo asked. 'Just you wanting to get value for money?'

'No, even at the beginning I wanted to be

sure that I kept you that long. A year down the road, otherwise, you could have decided to ditch me,' Gianni pointed out.

Her smooth brow furrowed as she struggled to accept that explanation. 'I was never going to ditch you...well, not unless you did something dreadful like murdering someone!' she extended. 'And even then, it would depend on the circumstances... Gosh, I've got it bad for you.'

'I feel so lucky.' Gianni had a huge smile on his lean dark features and a rare look of relaxation.

'That news I mentioned a few minutes ago,' Jo said abruptly. 'I'm pregnant.'

'Pregnant?' Gianni sat up to exclaim in shock.

'I hate to be the one to be telling you this,' Jo teased in a whisper, 'but what we've been doing tends to lead to conception.'

'I know that!' Gianni laughed, his eyes glinting with pleasure, and then he stretched out a hand to rest his fingers gently across her stomach. 'You feel the same.'

'You'll have to wait a while for anything to show.'

'It's magical. Everything I want all at once. A wife, a family, a child. You're amazing,'

Gianni told her with fierce conviction. 'You love me and you're pregnant.'

'A child is likely to mean a lot of changes in our lives,' she warned.

'I'm good with change now,' Gianni declared.

Jo began to unbutton his shirt, revealing his glorious muscular chest inch by inch. She felt so happy that she was vaguely surprised that she wasn't floating.

'Do you think you'll stay in love?' she heard herself ask and almost winced at that need for reassurance grabbing her.

'I do. I'm a lot older and wiser than I was the first time around. But I was hurt after my mother passed and then Fliss…as well,' he framed wryly. 'I honestly believed that I could protect myself from falling in love again but then the right woman appears, the one who keeps on catching your eye and surprising you, and, all of a sudden, falling in love is the most wonderful thing in the world.'

'Fliss couldn't have been similar to Fiona,' Jo guessed.

'No, Fliss was quiet and a little shy and very kind, but I'm bright enough to accept now that if she hadn't been ill, we wouldn't have stayed together so long. She never disagreed with me. She thought everything I did was fantastic.'

'I'm not like that.'

'We were too young, and university isn't the real world.' He sighed. 'I wasn't ready for such a major commitment, but I did love her.'

'I'm sure you did.' Jo removed his cufflinks and tugged down the sleeves of his shirt. 'But I know I've grown up a lot since I was a student.'

Gianni kicked off his shoes and peeled off his socks. 'I'm so comfortable with you. I've never had that with a woman.'

'Comfortable like an old armchair that's been worn in?' Jo scoffed.

'No…' Gianni tugged her down to him. 'I can just be myself and if I'm grouchy, you'll complain.'

'Darned right I will,' Jo interposed, running an appreciative hand down over his ridged abdomen, skimming his waistband, tracing the zip. 'I'm feeling much more confident now.'

'Will I survive the night?' Highly amused, Gianni lay back with a flourish. 'I'm all yours.'

'Always,' she muttered, the upswell of emotion threatening to overwhelm her. 'I love you. I need you.'

'I love and need you too, Jojo,' he groaned with pleasure.

EPILOGUE

Jo STOOD OUTSIDE Ladymead and simply savoured the view of the old Tudor house with the glow of lights behind the mullioned windows. It had taken five years and there had been many problems along the way but the house was finally finished. Temporary repairs had ultimately given way to a full restoration once the various permissions were granted and finally it was finished. The fantastic skyline of the house with its parade of elaborate chimneys and little turrets made her smile fondly. Repointed, the ornamental brickwork looked fabulous.

'Was it worth marrying you-know-who for?' her great-aunt Sybil whispered from behind her.

'So worth it, I'm dizzy thinking about it!' Jo laughed, turning round to see the older woman clad in a long emerald-green gown.

'Your costume is spectacular,' Sybil commented at the sight of the younger woman garbed like a Tudor queen.

'You look amazing, Sybil.'

'You don't think it's a bit mutton dressed as lamb?' Sybil asked with a grimace.

'Not a bit of it. You've got the looks and the figure and, for goodness' sake,' Jo chided, 'you're not so old that you have to be thinking that way!'

Sybil grinned. 'I knew you'd sort me out.'

'Is he planning to ask you tonight?'

Sybil went pink. 'I think so. He's been going on so much about what a special night this is and I can't think why our celebration party for Ladymead should be special for him in the same way it is for us.'

'Federico is a law unto himself.' Jo sighed, confident that Sybil's hopes would be met with a marriage proposal.

The changes through the last five years paraded at speed through Jo's brain. She had become a mother twice over, or maybe three times over since the first set had been twins, non-identical, a boy and a girl called Lorenzo and Alice, now lively four-year-olds. Trixie had been unbearable over her accurate prediction until Sybil pointed out that the twins weren't that surprising an arrival when Jo's mother and her uncle had been twins. Their toddler, Gabriele, had been more unexpected. Not a planned pregnancy, that last one, although Gabriele was such an adorable little boy nobody wanted to hand him back. The twins were dark of hair and eye, like Gianni, but Gabriele was blond like his mother, with big brown eyes, a mixture of both parents.

Fiona never had come back to work at Ladymead. Gianni continued to have a business connection with her firm but little personal contact. Sybil had taken over supervision of the work with Federico showing great interest and proffering advice.

'He's weaselling his way into her affections,' Gianni had said uncharitably when, near the end of that first year, Sybil finally agreed to a dinner date with his father.

Two years later, Gianni's tune had changed. 'He's totally gone on her. I hope she doesn't hurt him. He's surprisingly sensitive.'

Jo counted the transformation of her husband's relationship with his father her biggest success. It had taken a long time and an abundance of tact for Gianni to accept that his mother might not have been as honest as she could have been about her marriage. But once he had realised how the marriage had functioned from his father's point of view he had been gutted when he had to look back at his mother through the lens of an adult. Ever since that evening when the two men had talked in depth, Gianni had dropped his guard with his father, invited him into their lives and begun talking to him as the parent Federico was. Federico had been too strict a parent and he was well aware of the mistakes he had made.

'Let's go in...' Sybil tucked a hand in the crook of Jo's arm. 'This is so exciting! Parties at both houses and Ladymead finally alive again!'

'Where's Gianni?' Sybil asked.

'He'll be back in time. He promised,' Jo said confidently, because Gianni always kept his promises.

'That jewellery is breathtaking.' Sybil sighed enviously, touching a finger to the ruby and diamond necklace and drop earrings her great-niece wore. 'Isabella's collection...right?'

'Yes, no need to buy much with that collection in the safe,' Jo quipped. 'You can borrow it for special occasions. Gianni wouldn't mind.'

'But Federico wouldn't like me wearing anything that belonged to her,' Sybil replied wryly. 'Thanks, but no, thanks.'

They strolled into the great hall with its medieval screens and minstrels' gallery. Jo peered up at the decorative hammerbeam open timber roof, which had been freshly picked out in the original Elizabethan colours. Tapestries she had forgotten once hung at Ladymead now adorned the walls again. Subtle light glowed in corners as catering staff hovered to offer them drinks. Everyone local as well as their friends and Gianni's business acquaintances had been invited. Belvedere offered a rather different level of hospitality with the ballroom and a buffet and loads of seating for a crowd. Ladymead was still primarily a family house, a beautiful one but not a grand one, Jo reflected fondly, wandering through the restored rooms with growing pleasure.

Her biggest surprise in the five years of her marriage had been Gianni telling her that he had a temperature-controlled warehouse storing every valuable article that had ever been sold from Ladymead. Apparently, the Renzettis had begun buying those items when his grandfather was a young man and his father had continued the purchases, as had Gianni. Thus, the priceless original oak trestle table and benches and the tapestries and the family portraits were now in place again. There was a valuable Chinese vase restored to the tiny, wainscoted library and a few precious old books, as well as a couple of oak four-poster beds now returned to the main bedrooms. The warehouse had proved to be an Aladdin's cave and none of the articles had ever crossed the threshold of Belvedere, not being deemed suitable for the grandeur of the Edwardian mansion.

'The Renzettis had a plan to take over your family home for many, many years,' Gianni had explained with a grimace. 'And just think, all I had to do was marry you!'

'Smartass,' she had teased back. 'But I'm really grateful that all these items can come back where they belong. If your family hadn't bought them, they would have been lost for ever.'

Her grandmother was sitting in the library.

Never keen on large gatherings, she was relying on her sisters and her granddaughter to do the honours. None of them minded because the older woman had had a heart attack the year before and only surgery and a very strict diet in the aftermath had returned her to health. These days, she promised to take it easy but was regularly to be found cooking at Belvedere because she was great friends with their housekeeper and very fond of Gianni and his father.

McTavish was no longer at Jo's heel. Age had given him arthritis and he only left his basket at home if tempted by food. Fairy was older too but no less graceful and quiet. A labradoodle had also come into Sybil's rescue barn. Ace was the twins' dog because Lorenzo and Alice had fallen madly in love with the fluffy puppy of indeterminate parentage. Duffy had stayed with them, loving a household where there was an almost constant audience. Lorenzo was trying to teach him rap and make him less of an 'oldie' because Duffy's biblical and Shakespearean quotes were meaningless to a four-year-old.

Gianni and Federico, clad in smart dinner jackets, walked through the arched front entrance together and Jo grinned while her heart leapt at the sight of her husband. She hadn't lost an atom of her susceptibility to those spectacular dark good looks of his.

He accepted the glass offered to him and did a double take at his wife, garbed in her very elaborate Elizabethan silk and brocade embroidered costume. 'You take my breath away, *cara*.'

'The kids are all in bed,' she warned him.

'I thought you'd surrender and let them come.'

'No, there's too many strangers about *and* the lake. They're too young and adventurous to be trusted.' She sighed with regret.

Gianni groaned. 'Their nanny's bringing them. It's a big night. I thought you'd want them to enjoy the experience.'

He was the fun parent and she was the stricter one. It had never occurred to her that that was how they would turn out as parents. Lorenzo hurtled across the room. 'Mum… where's the fireworks?' he demanded.

'The fireworks won't be happening until ten, which is two hours away,' Gianni told his disappointed son.

'Fireworks.' Alice ground out the word

with disdain. 'I want to see everybody admiring our house.'

'She's so like you it's ridiculous,' Gianni whispered fondly, closing his free hand over Jo's and even that small connection sent a quiver of awareness through her.

Gabriele left their nanny, Janessa, to seek out his mother. He grabbed a handful of her gown to keep her within reach and sucked his thumb happily, almost tottering with the exhaustion he was fighting off.

Sybil whispered in her ear, 'We'll keep the kiddoes here tonight with the nanny. He still doesn't think far ahead. It's your wedding anniversary. You deserve a child-free night.'

Jo turned round but her great-aunt had already moved away.

'Happy anniversary,' Gianni breathed tautly. 'Guess I blew it again with the kids. Sybil doesn't whisper as quietly as she thinks she does.'

'The twins will be fine here for the night with Trixie and Gran.' Jo gave him a serene smile. 'Has it occurred to you that I've now done my five-year sentence in marriage?'

His hand jerked on hers and he turned her

round to face him. 'If I thought you meant that, I'd lock you up sooner than lose you.'

Jo leant dangerously close and feathered her lips across his cheek. 'I hope you're planning to lock yourself up with me.'

Fire smouldered in his very intent gaze, black lashes like fans low. 'Anything you want, you get.'

'I like it when you're…ruthless,' she selected softly.

Lorenzo yanked at her gown. 'Mum! What's Grandad doing? He's being weird!'

'*Madonna mia…*' Gianni groaned half under his breath. 'How could he embarrass himself like that?'

Jo looked past him and saw her father-in-law down on one knee extending a ring box while Sybil stood there frozen between pleasure and terror. 'He's asking Auntie Sybil to marry him and I think it's very romantic. He even brought a photographer to record the moment,' she explained calmly.

'You *knew* about this?' Gianni demanded.

'He needed my help to choose the ring.'

'And you didn't let me in on the secret?'

'No. He trusted me to keep it quiet.'

She watched Sybil slide the ring onto her

finger as a champagne toast was offered to the happy couple.

'At least she didn't say no.' Gianni sighed in relief. 'Because with Sybil you never quite know. You share that trait for the unexpected.'

'I think we need to take Gabriele home and tuck him into bed,' Jo told her husband gently, not wishing to sound critical. 'And greet our guests at Belvedere while we're there.'

Gianni stooped to pick up Gabriele, who was already half asleep. 'I thought he would have more staying power.'

'He's still a baby.'

'If we're going home, while we're upstairs,' Gianni began thickly, 'we—'

'No, you'll have to wait until after the fireworks,' Jo told him with some satisfaction.

As they drove back to the house, the original gate having developed into a proper roadway to the rear of Ladymead, connecting the two houses, Jo thought blissfully of how happy she was with just her family. She still helped out Sybil, Trixie and her grandmother and took a continued interest in the community but she had bags of time to spend with Gianni. They often went horse riding on the estate. He had bought her a splendid Arab mare for their anniversary. They travelled together and often took weekends away at his other properties.

'You promised me for ever and ever,' Gianni reminded her as she tucked Gabriele into bed.

Jo laughed. 'You couldn't get rid of me even if you tried!'

His stunning dark golden eyes glittered over her lovely face with intense appreciation. 'I'm crazy about you too, *cara*.'

As he caught her to him and kissed her breathless before she could even protest, her body went liquid in his embrace, the sexual heat that only he could awaken sending an arrow of hunger through her. 'Stop it…we have to go down,' she scolded him.

'If I have to wait until after the fireworks, I'll be expecting quite an experience,' he warned her with a slow-burning smile of sensual intent.

Jo tilted her head to one side and skimmed a playful forefinger across one high cheekbone. 'Well, I don't like to boast—'

He grabbed her at the top of the stairs and held her tight, which was quite an achievement with the voluminous skirts of her costume. 'I love you so much, Jojo…'

'And you show me that love every day, which is why I'm insanely, deeply in love with you too,' she declared with a luminous smile before they went downstairs hand in hand to greet their guests.

* * * * *

Were you swept away by the drama in
The Italian's Bride Worth Billions?
Then make sure you don't miss these other captivating stories by Lynne Graham!

Cinderella's Desert Baby Bombshell
Her Best Kept Royal Secret
Promoted to the Greek's Wife
The Heirs His Housekeeper Carried
The King's Christmas Heir

Available now!